THE HIRONO CHRONICLES

MEERA

THOMAS JOHN HOWARD BOGGIS

MARKOSIA

FIRST PRINTING, September 2020.
Harry Markos, Director.

Paperback: ISBN 978-1-913359-98-0
eBook: ISBN 978-1-913359-99-7

Book design by: Ian Sharman

Cover art and world map by: Mark Gerrard

Editor: Stephen Davis

www.markosia.com

First Edition

"To my mum and dad for their endless love and support, my brothers, sister, brother-in-law and nephews for always being there and my dog Dodge for just being him."

PROLOGUE

I remember the first battle as though I had been there myself. It was described to me so vividly that I still dream of it at night. In my dreams I stand beside them, comrades in arms, and fight against the barbarians; fight against hatred and cruelty and malice… and greed.

Innumerable bonfires blazed in the semi-darkness along the undulating hillsides like shooting stars fallen to earth, the flames swaying in a chill westerly wind. Shjin Kitano surveyed them dispassionately as he strode up and down the serried ranks of Kurai warriors who stood tall and proud, longbows or spears clutched tightly in their hands, their eyes fixed on the flickering pools of flame.

Shjin came to a stop and turned his head to look out eastward across the dark flatland of the Hirono domain. The sky overhead was a furnace of colour and the jagged teeth of the mountains bit into the horizon. A bad omen some would say, but for who?

A rugged-looking man in his late thirties, Shjin was a formidable warrior, his somewhat slight size belying his true strength. His hair hung loose around his shoulders and his stubbly jaws tensed as his teeth clenched together. Beneath his red leather breastplate, which was embossed with a curious crest, he wore a faded scarlet kimono and around his waist he wore a kilt of plated steel buckled in place with a studded belt of black leather. A pair of gauntlets covered his wrists, plated too with high-polished steel that bore many intricate designs and symbols. At his left side two swords hung horizontally from his belt, their black scabbards gleaming dully.

Shjin turned slowly on the spot and headed back down the line, surveying each man as he passed. Their attire was not dissimilar to his own, although many of the warriors had personalised their armour with engravings of their family crests.

Even though Shjin was an officer he did not dress differently from the ordinary foot soldiers. Even as he was promoted up through the ranks he continued to dress as they did and it was this air of humility that commanded the respect of his men.

Upon reaching the end of the line Shjin stopped and raised his head. He sniffed the air and his grip tightened on the handle of the sword sheathed at his side. Turning to a man standing near him he spoke in an undertone so that none but his friend could hear.

'I can smell the filth, Tay; they're standing in the darkness behind the fires, biding their time, waiting for the sun to rise high enough and blind us before they attack.' Tay Asaki squinted his eyes and peered into the darkness, then nodded silently in agreement with Shjin.

A ripple spread through the ranks of Kurai warriors as each one tensed suddenly, grasping their weapons tighter and listening intently. It was then that Shjin heard it too. Ahead of them, in the pool of shadow behind the fires, a faint sound could be heard, its volume increasing with every second.

Clack! Clack! Clack!

'They're getting ready to attack,' Tay whispered to Shjin. 'We must move now before they have the sun to their advantage.' Grabbing a helmet from the floor, Shjin strapped it on to his head and raised a flag to signal a man at the other end of the line who raised his flag in response. Slowly, the Kurai warriors began to advance across the darkened flatlands, their weapons held high and the archers notching arrows to bow strings.

Clack! Clack! Clack! Clack!

The chilling sound filled the air for miles around, its intensity nearing fever pitch. When the ranks of advancing warriors were halfway toward the blazing fires, they began to notice dark shapes emerging ahead of them to stand silhouetted against the flames. Raising a flag, Shjin drew his warriors to a halt in a shallow dip in the landscape. The shadowy figures had their weapons raised high and were beating them against their helmeted heads to create their ominous build up to battle, their faces taut with pain.

Suddenly, every one of them lowered their weapons as though at a signal and an intense silence fell across the flatlands. The silence lasted only momentarily as a hulking figure stepped forward into the firelight and levelled his weapon at the Kurai warriors. His face appeared hideously distorted; the barbaric features surmounted by a helmet with two large spikes at its top. The man's voice rang out across the flatlands as he screamed a single word in a harsh, guttural language:

'Geikou!'

'Down! Everybody down!' Shjin screamed at his men. The Kurai army barely had chance to move as flaming arrows rained out of the sky, thudding into the earth all around them, many shafts extinguishing their flames in the flesh of men. Shjin was the first one up, his sword raised high above his head, roaring at his men to attack.

Together, the Kurai warriors surged across the flatlands as the sun appeared fully above the distant mountains, dispelling the last of the darkness. Running almost blindly now, the warriors rushed onwards, the blood thumping through their veins. Beside him, Shjin watched as an arrow took a comrade through the eye; watched as his body crumpled limply to the earth and rolled to a stop in the damp grass.

The two sides clashed then, steel ringing on steel, the awful sound of combat tearing out across the flats. Hacking and slashing with fierce energy,

Shjin cut a swathe through his enemies, their blood mingling with the dew on the grass. An arrow thudded into his shoulder and he sank to his knees, his body heaving with exertion as the battle raged all around him. Tugging the arrow out, Shjin's face split into a wolfish grin. Getting quickly to his feet he threw himself back into the fray as the shadows diminished and the sun climbed ever higher in the morning sky.

CHAPTER ONE

As the battle raged and men fought and died, far away, deep within the mountains, my friend Kamari was in trouble. When he later recounted the events of his journey, he had difficulty doing so, and now... so do I. But I will do my best to relay his story exactly as he described it.

Driving snow obscured their vision and an icy wind whistled past their numb faces as they struggled blindly through the snow, their leaden limbs slowing them down. They had become hopelessly lost when the snow hit as they were trying to cross the mountains but, as hope dwindled, they knew they had no choice but to continue. With their strength waning they searched fruitlessly for a shelter against the elements but none was forthcoming and so they continued on; three dark smudges against a pure white canvas.

The small family huddled together as they moved; trying to retain what little body heat they had. The figure standing at their centre was a stocky boy, a little over fifteen winters old. His shoulder length dark hair whipped around his face as he looked at the person to his left and said, through chattering teeth:

'We must be nearly across by now, Mama.' His mother looked over at the boy's father, her aging face stricken with worry, and saw the same look on her husband's face. She hugged her son tighter and replied with an enthusiasm she did not feel:

'Yes, I'm sure we are, Kamari.'

For many hours they trudged onward through the snow and as night fell visibility dramatically lessened and the temperature plummeted still further.

Kamari noticed his mother beginning to lag behind and clutched her hand to pull her close. Her fingers felt like ice as their hands locked together. Kamari's father saw that his wife was in trouble and rushed over to her. Her breath was coming in short, sharp bursts but she managed to gasp out:

'I need to... I need to stop, just for a moment.' They stopped dead, the snow already past their knees, and hunkered down together. His parents hugged each other close and Kamari found himself locked between them in a tight embrace.

He could not say how long they stayed there as the snow built up around them, for time no longer had any meaning for Kamari in that blank and featureless landscape. Sleep began to overtake him and he found it hard to resist the temptation to slip into its welcome darkness, but in these freezing temperatures he knew it would be death to do so.

But soon he could no longer fight it; his eyelids were like lead weights and he felt himself slipping away. A noise to his left brought him back to consciousness and he realised that someone was close by.

'Mama, Papa, someone's here,' he croaked as a shadow fell over him. He felt his parents' grip on his body lessen and as it did darkness enveloped him and he felt the cold no longer.

CHAPTER TWO

In my bed, a world away from vicious battles and freezing mountaintops, I lay quiet and still, alone with my thoughts.

The room swam before my bleary gaze, my eyes red rimmed and stinging, as I dozily surveyed the area around me for the umpteenth time. The wooden walls and floor creaked occasionally as someone in the house moved in their sleep and what little furnishing there was in the room was littered with books and scrolls. A weak shaft of light streamed in through a high window, picking out the individual motes of dust that hung lazily on the still air. Judging from the strength and angle of the light I could tell that it was early morning and looking around, I picked up the book I had let slip from my hand sometime earlier. It had fallen open on the chapter that described the history of our village's founders and it reminded me that today was an anniversary of the founding of our village, Aigano, in Kohaku Valley, many generations ago.

I rubbed my eyes and stretched, listening to my joints cracking successively. Yet another night had melded seamlessly with another day. Insomnia does that to you. When you are only able to snatch mere minutes of uncomfortable sleep each night you begin to lose track of time and place. I had suffered from this sleeping disorder from a very young age; stemming from the day over ten years ago when my grandfather was murdered in front of me. The image of his murderer still burned in my mind as I lay awake each night, as though it had imprinted itself on the backs of my eyes.

It was for this reason that the room was filled with many writings from times and ages past. I spent many hours each night reading up on the history of our domain, Hirono, and practicing my calligraphy until I could write in a fluid hand. Often, I would lose myself for hours in some fictional story, praying that I would fall asleep; but it never happened.

I heaved myself up from the thick straw mattress on the floor and stumbled over to the basin of water on the small table beneath the window. I splashed some water on to my face and dried it with a rough towel. Beside the window hung a mirror and I looked into it, surveying my reflection. A boy of fifteen summers looked back at me, a mop of untidy black hair veiling dark brown eyes that bore witness to many years of sleepless nights. The figure in the mirror was tall, although not unusually so, and was of a slight build, though evidence of some physical training was apparent. I almost did not recognise this figure in the mirror. It had changed so quickly over the last few months and years that he appeared like a stranger to me. In my near constant state halfway between asleep and awake, things often seemed strange and ethereal to me. At times I felt like a ghost, lost in a world in which I did not belong.

Next to the basin lay the last letter I had received from Kamari. It had been a long time since he had last written to me and I was beginning to get worried. The letter read:

Dear Takashi,

We have arrived safely at my uncle's house. The journey was long and difficult (so I can only imagine what it must be like when the snows hit) but considering there's absolutely nothing to do here I've got plenty of time to recuperate! I wish you were here too, there'd be all sorts of things we could do together but it's no fun without you. Don't think I'll be coming to uncle's house again next year (if I can avoid it). We should go off on an adventure together instead!

Anyway, I'll write to you again soon.

Kamari Shiro.

With a yawn I turned from the mirror and crossed the room, grabbing a pair of shin length cream trousers from a pile in the corner and pulling them on. Throwing on a dark blue kimono over the top and belting it loosely around my waist, I quietly headed towards the latticed screen door which I slid open before me and passed through.

Closing the door behind me I padded silently down the corridor to a side room that contained a small but intricately carved shrine, encircled by a ring of wavering candles.

After lighting some incense burners, I knelt down respectfully before the shrine and offered up a silent prayer to the Valley Spirit, asking his forgiveness for my failings and humbly requesting a good harvest and peaceful year for my family.

The room was small and badly ventilated and soon tendrils of thick incense smoke began to snake around my body and I started to feel light-headed. Sitting there alone in that small room with my head swimming and my eyes watering I recalled the last day I had spent with Kamari before he had travelled over the mountains with his parents to visit his aunt and uncle.

It had been on the Day of Lost Souls, when the inhabitants of Aigano offered up prayers for those they had lost and asked for their loved ones to rest peacefully in the afterlife. On this day a special ceremony was held for the ancestors of both my family and Kamari's, for it was they who founded Aigano village.

My ancestor, Timaeo Asano, and Kamari's ancestor, Deakami Shiro, had been great warriors of their age and had battled through many hardships to found our village. At first they had been well loved, and down through the generations the families in the village had greatly respected the Asano and Shiro families. However, in recent years times had been hard, harvests had been bad, and soon the respect that the Aigano villagers held for our families dwindled and died.

Two families in the village remained loyal to us but they had become like outcasts from the rest of the inhabitants. On the Day of Lost Souls the ceremony commemorating our ancestors had begun and the only people in attendance were the two small families - the Takami family and the Nariaka family.

I remembered what Kamari had said to me after the ceremony. His eyes had burned with fury as we headed back to our homes by the Daku River that cut southwards through the valley. I knew of Kamari's feelings on the lack of respect shown us by the villagers, but I had never seen him that angry before. His fists had been tightly clenched, his knuckles white, and when he spoke his voice had been laden with malice.

'How dare they display such insolence on this day, this day! Our ancestors built this village from the ground up, gave their families a place to live, gave them a future! And this is how they show their respect!' He spat bitterly on the floor. 'By not even showing up at the ceremony, let alone offering up their prayers! They dishonour themselves by not showing their loyalty to our families!' I had wanted to say that we no longer commanded their respect because we personally had done nothing to earn it. Having an ancestor that had done great things did not entitle us to the same respect they had received, but I had seen Kamari in these moods before and I kept silent.

A sound brought me back to the present. I realised that I had been at the shrine for many hours and my family were just waking up. I lit a candle and placed it before the shrine then bowed low and touched my head to the floor. I still felt groggy from the incense fumes and lack of sleep and did not feel like talking to my parents just now. So, without a sound, I left the shrine and walked down the corridor to the door that led outside.

Once outside a wave of sound washed over me as I surveyed the world around me from the doorstep. Our house was built on the lower slopes of the steep sided valley, just before it ran into the western river bank. Kamari's house was away to my left on the same side of the river, although his house was built higher up on the valley slopes. To the northeast of our house an ornate wooden bridge spanned the river at its thinnest point providing access to the main area of the village. From where I stood the sound of the Daku River reached my ears, the rushing water whipping itself up into foam as it passed over jutting rocks. Looking across the river I could see the far side of the valley, its slopes densely covered in maple and cedar trees. From this distance the treetops looked like a heaving green sea as a strong southerly wind swept across them.

I stepped into my sandals and headed towards the bridge that would take me to the eastern bank. Looking down into the water I watched as the shimmering, silvery body of a fish whipped past me down river, the wind chasing little ripples after it.

Once on the other bank I wandered towards the village, taking in the sights around me as I did so. The many small wooden houses were built around a large open clearing where most of the festivities took place. At the north end of the village, where the valley started to peter out into low rolling hills, was the cemetery and public shrine, which were visited each day by the villagers. Next to these were the training grounds, where the men and boys of the village were trained in the art of weapons and horsemanship. At the southern end of the village, south east from my home, were the rice paddies, fruit trees and animal paddocks that provided the villagers with food. But even from here it was obvious that the harvest was looking bad.

Walking through the village I noticed that preparations were under way for the anniversary of Aigano, but it was obvious to me they were being done without any real conviction. Areas had been set up where young ones could play games and tables had been laid out for the feast, but the banners were hung limply and bore none of the wonderful designs of previous celebrations in times past. As I passed through the village I noticed faces peering out at me from darkened windows, the expressions cold and menacing, quickly vanishing if I turned to look at them. This feeling of hostility grew ever stronger as I passed the houses until I could stand it no longer and turned back towards my home.

As I was passing a house on the outer edge of the village, I felt the gaze of someone upon me, but it did not seem to be one of aggression. Turning to look I noticed a young girl, about my age, looking at me through the window. She waved shyly as my eyes fell upon her then she disappeared back into the house. I recognised her as Mei Nariaka, the daughter of Takeda Nariaka who was head of one of the two families still loyal to the Asano and Shiro families. I held great respect for their family; that they should honour the old ways even in the face of the other villagers' scorn for them.

Yawning mightily, I continued homewards. As I crossed the bridge that led to the west bank, I noticed the water sparkling like myriad diamonds in the morning light. I stopped briefly to marvel at this sight then wove my way back home.

Kicking off my sandals I slid the door open and passed inside and soon heard the sound of clinking bowls from the dining room. My family were kneeling around the low table eating sweetened gruel sprinkled with berries, my mother and father on one side and my young sister Mia on the other. As I entered the room my mother and Mia both looked up but my father continued eating, his face creased in an expression of deep thought.

'Good morning dear,' my mother said, as I knelt on the floor by the table and picked up my bowl of gruel. 'Did you manage to get any sleep last night?' she added kindly.

'No, not really,' I replied, as I spooned down my meal. 'I was… reading.'

'You must have read nearly all the books in there by now,' she answered as she started clearing up the bowls, her long, dark hair swishing around as she moved, its length unable to hide the lines that were slowly creeping across her face, the visible results of both age and worry.

'Yes, I have,' I replied. 'But I've started reading them again.' As she turned to take the bowls away, I noticed her expression as she looked at me. It was one of sympathy, possibly tinged with sorrow. Before I had time to fathom the meaning of this my father looked up at me as though coming out of a dream.

'Oh, hello Takashi, didn't hear you come in,' he said. 'Did you get any sleep last night?' With a sigh I turned to my father.

'No, not really,' I answered.

'Did that tea I gave you not help?' he asked, absent-mindedly stroking his short, dark beard which I noticed was streaked with grey.

'It made me feel drowsy but I didn't fall asleep.'

'Well, I'm sure you'll grow out of this sleep problem,' he replied offhandedly.

'Yes… maybe,' I answered.

My mother came back into the room holding something in her hand.

'Oh Takashi, I forgot to mention,' she said. 'This letter came for you while you were out this morning. I think it's from Kamari.' I took the letter from her eagerly and found that it was written on a small piece of parchment, probably delivered by some kind of carrier bird. Kamari's spidery script was instantly recognisable as he always chose to ignore the traditional bold style of writing. The letter was dated over a week ago which led me to believe that the carrier must have been blown off course, causing the delivery to take longer than expected.

Dear Takashi,

Sorry I haven't written for a while but things have been hectic here recently. We have been unable to cross the mountains because of fears of being caught in a snowstorm, but the weather seems to have improved and we are setting off for home any day now. Father says that we should be back in time for the anniversary, but don't hold your breath.

Hope to see you soon.

Kamari Shiro.

With a leap of excitement, I realised that as the letter was dated over a week ago Kamari could be back here at any minute. With renewed vigour I joined my family in preparing for that night's celebrations.

CHAPTER THREE

A dull throbbing pain in his head was the first thing Kamari became aware of as the mist of his fever partially cleared and he was able to open his eyes. He felt cold, even though his body was tightly wrapped in a blanket, and slowly he took in the room around him, his eyesight blurred and unsteady. The room seemed small and sparsely furnished and through the window he could dimly see the outlines of the mountains to the north, set against the inky canopy of the night sky. Judging from their nearness he could tell that he had not moved too far from the mountain pass he could last remember.

It was then that the memories came flooding in of that terrible journey and at once his thoughts flew to his parents. Where were they? What had happened to them? Why had they chanced crossing the mountains in such bad weather? These thoughts pulsed inside his brain, bringing with them a gnawing feeling of dread that he could not explain.

He sat up quickly on his mat, causing his head to pound worse than ever, and frantically scanned the room for any sign of his parents. Blood throbbed in his temples and he began to feel light-headed, forcing him to lie back. As he did so he heard footsteps outside the door and muffled voices, their tone low and worried. The words were indistinguishable but soon a hazy figure appeared in the doorway and strode towards him, followed by two others.

From his prone position Kamari looked dazedly at the nearest of them and at last the figure spoke, his voice full of concern.

'How do you feel?' A cold shiver ran through Kamari's body and for a moment it felt like he was back in the snow and again the memories began rushing around inside his head. He wanted to speak, to ask this person where his parents were, but the words seemed to stick in his throat and he found that he could not answer.

A confused look crossed the man's face when he did not reply.

'The man and woman we found you with… your parents?' Again, Kamari found that he could not reply. He merely looked up at the man, fear and confusion in his eyes. The man glanced over at the other two figures and whispered, 'A mute, perhaps?' They did not respond and simply looked on with quiet intensity. Turning back, the man spoke again to Kamari, his words clearer and more pronounced.

'I am sorry to say that both the man and the woman… died before our patrol arrived. At first we feared you were dead too but somehow… they managed to save you by shielding you with their bodies.' A lump swelled up in Kamari's throat and the backs of his eyes prickled as tears formed there. Grief swept throughout his body, bringing with it a strange numbness that pervaded every inch of him. He turned onto his side, away from the people watching him, and shut his eyes to prevent the tears from falling. Quietly, the three figures left the room, shutting the door carefully behind them. Once they had left Kamari opened his eyes and let his sorrow pour out, his body racked by silent sobs. For many hours he lay alone on his mat as the darkness slowly ebbed away and sleep finally overtook.

For several days Kamari lay without moving, his fever initially worsening as grief weakened him. Twice a day someone came in with a tray of food and left it on the low table by his bed. Each time they would tell him to take the beaker of medicine with the food to ease his fever, but he could not answer and just lay with his back to them, staring out of the window. He began to differentiate between the people bringing his food simply by their footsteps as they approached along the corridor. The young girl, the older woman; they appeared to take it in turns to visit his room.

Time passed slowly as he lay there on the fourth day, wrestling with his grief and trying to remember why they had risked the journey across the mountains. But gradually his strength began to return and soon he ventured over to the window to view his surroundings. He appeared to be in a large fortified village a few miles from the foot of the Northern Mountains. Through the window he could see a sturdy looking wooden stockade that ran all around the village, its top patrolled by armed soldiers. Many single floored wooden houses were dotted haphazardly around the village with a central shrine that the villagers visited regularly. The three bells of the shrine rang out mournfully twice daily, summoning its inhabitants to morning and evening prayers. On his first night in the village the sound of the bells had reminded Kamari to pray for a peaceful journey for his parents' souls, in the hope that they would not linger in this world and would pass without mishap to the next.

By the morning of the fifth day Kamari felt that the fever had finally passed. He got up and dressed in the simple cream kimono he had been provided with. A chill draft blew through the room and he grabbed the sheet from the mat, wrapping it around his shoulders to shield himself from the cold. Falteringly he headed towards the door and slid it open, not bothering to close it behind him. At the far end of the corridor was a room from which voices issued, their tone light and friendly.

When he reached the door, Kamari tentatively knocked and awaited a response. The voices within ceased almost instantly and a jovial looking young man slid the door open before him. With a smile and a wave, he ushered Kamari into the room and shut the door behind them.

'Come in, come in, are you feeling better now?' Instantly Kamari realised this was the same man who had told him of his parents' death, but he still found he could not respond. It was as though there was some blockage in his throat, preventing the flow of words and all he could manage was to silently open his mouth. The same confused look crossed the man's face and he looked over at the people around him. Kneeling around a low table were a woman, clearly the man's wife, and two young girls of about Kamari's age. They had been eating rice with a sweetened plum sauce, their bowls forgotten as they looked at Kamari.

The young man turned back to him and asked, 'Can you understand what I am saying?' Kamari nodded and a smile spread across the man's face. 'Were you able to talk before... before we found you?' Again, Kamari nodded and watched as relief crossed his face. Turning to his wife the man said:

'It must have been the grief and the fever that caused him to lose his voice. It'll probably return in a few days.' Turning back to Kamari he asked, 'What is your name? Can you write it down?' Kamari nodded and took the charcoal and parchment the man gave him, swiftly scrawling his name in his short spidery script.

'Kamari Shiro,' the man said, looking at him with a smile. 'I am Mauru Hitai. This is my wife Sen and our daughters Chiro and Akayama,' he continued, pointing at each one in turn. Kamari nodded at each of them then turned his attention back to Mauru.

'Come, sit and eat with us,' he said, indicating a space at the table next to his own. 'The maids tell me that you have eaten very little since you arrived so you must be famished.'

Kamari ate hungrily as he listened to Mauru who spoke at length about the village and the people that lived there. It turned out the village Kamari found himself in was called Kirina and was an outpost of the great Harakima castle in the south east. They had been under the protection of Harakima's ruler, Lord Orran, for decades and had worked in conjunction with him throughout many of the most decisive battles of the last thirty years. Kamari knew little of Harakima himself, not being given to the reading of books. But thinking about it brought to mind his best friend Takashi who had always been interested in the history of that place. Kamari also discovered that Mauru was the son of Kirina's lord and a highly respected man in the village.

When Kamari had finished his food, Mauru stood up from the table and gestured towards the door.

'Follow me and I will give you a tour of the village,' he said as he slid the door open.

The sky outside was overcast, gradually turning a steely grey as dark storm clouds began to amass over the village. A light wind ruffled their clothes as they stepped into their sandals on the covered wooden veranda that ran around the house. Looking out at the village Kamari noticed just how much it resembled Aigano, especially the houses and the way they were laid out around a central meeting area. He bit his lip; thinking about home had hammered the memories back to the forefront of his mind and he found it hard to suppress them, but he did not want to show emotions in front of this unfamiliar lord.

He looked away from Mauru to hide his eyes, out westwards across the village that bore so many similarities to his home. Most of the houses were simple but sturdy one floor buildings, made almost entirely of wood, their roofs conical and thatched, testament to the skill of those who had built them. Thick grass covered the land as far as he could see, except for the dirt paths connecting the buildings with each other and the large central clearing where the shrine stood and all the village meetings were held.

Kamari started as Mauru stepped up behind him and looked out at the village.

'It isn't the nicest of weather, but I will show you around while it holds out.'

Mauru led Kamari around the village, pointing out areas of interest such as the stables, the shrine and the large ornate well that drew its water from the mountain rivers running beneath the ground. They also passed the main gates at the southern end of the village as Mauru took Kamari to the far west side where the animals were kept and the rice paddies and fruit trees grew.

As they moved around the village Kamari watched as people appeared in their doorways or stopped what they were doing and bowed low, touching their heads to the ground murmuring, "Lord Mauru". Kamari wanted to speak then, to tell Mauru about the state of Aigano and the dissent of the villagers, but still found that words would not come. He felt sure that Mauru would know of his legendary ancestor Deakami Shiro, and was certain that if these villagers knew who he was they would be bowing to him, not just to Mauru. Anger welled up inside him as he thought of the Aigano villagers who no longer showed loyalty to his or Takashi's families; who dared to openly display their disobedience by not showing up on the Day of Lost Souls.

However, his anger abated as Mauru led him to the stables and showed him the many fine horses he and his father possessed. One particular horse stood out above the rest. He was dark brown in colour, with a thick black mane and tail and a single white stripe that ran down his long and noble nose.

'That is Dagri, he is my favourite horse and the most stunning example of his kind,' he said, noticing where Kamari was looking. 'He was given to me by Lord Orran a few years ago as a reward for my services to him. Would you like to ride him? He has quite a nervous temperament but I'm sure he will let you.' Kamari nodded emphatically and with a smile

Mauru turned towards the equipment rack where the saddles and riding gear hung.

As he was pulling a saddle down a messenger arrived in the doorway of the stable, bowing low to the floor.

'Lord Mauru, Lord Hanare would like to see you and the boy as soon as possible.'

Turning back to Kamari with a sigh, Mauru apologised, 'I am sorry Kamari, but it looks like you will have to ride Dagri another time. It is best not to keep my father waiting; he is a very impatient man.'

At the northern edge of the village stood by far the grandest building Kamari had yet seen. It appeared almost palatial to an eye unaccustomed to such finery. It stood as a dramatic contrast to the simple thatched buildings of the villagers, towering above them, at least three floors in height. Its roof was roughly triangular in shape, sweeping and tiled in blood red, with each tier of the building marked by a kind of jutting tiled roof, adding to the overall grandeur of its appearance. The covered veranda that ran around the building was supported by many beautifully carved pillars that bore the likenesses of dragons and warriors.

Noticing the awed look on Kamari's face, Mauru smiled and said, 'My father enjoys the finer things. He believes that lords should live much more comfortably than the common folk. Me on the other hand... I prefer a simple life. Follow me inside.'

Mauru led the way up the steps and, after removing his sandals, entered the building with Kamari following swiftly behind.

As they entered, a servant greeted them, bowing low and touching his head to the floor before Mauru's feet.

'Please stand up,' Mauru said, barely disguising his exasperation. The servant remained prone, keeping his eyes fixed on the floor, and said, 'Lord Mauru, Lord Hanare will see you immediately in the tea room.' The man crawled backwards toward the door, keeping his prostrate position, and slid it open, gesturing for them to enter. Sighing deeply Mauru stepped through the doorway and into the room, with Kamari following hesitantly behind.

Kamari knew the correct etiquette for meeting with lords, although he had never had the pleasure. The Aigano villagers had shown him this courtesy in the early years of his life before the dissent had begun and he had, like every child, been taught the procedure at a young age. However, he managed to snatch a quick glimpse of the Lord before he knelt on the ground before him, touching his head to the floor. He stayed in the same position, knowing that it was high bad manners to stand up without being asked to by the lord.

He felt resentful at having to defer to Hanare. He came from a strong and respected bloodline and at the least he should be on the same level as this man seated before him. But he remained prostrate, as this lord was unlikely to recognise him and he knew the power that such men wielded.

For a few moments Lord Hanare said nothing and Kamari could feel his eyes boring into the back of his head. Then at once he spoke. His voice was deep and slightly tremulous, which gave away his age.

'Who have you brought before me, Mauru? I hear one of our patrols found him.'

'Yes, father, his name is Kamari,' Mauru answered. 'Our patrol found him while on a routine sweep of the mountain pass. His parents died in the extreme cold when they attempted to cross the mountains.'

'Did they indeed? The fools…' Lord Hanare said, quietly. Kamari clenched his teeth in anger and narrowly avoided responding. 'Why did they try to cross the mountains in such bad weather?'

'I'm not sure, father.'

'Well, haven't you asked him yet?' Hanare said impatiently. 'You, boy, why did your family try to cross the mountains?' Mauru swiftly intervened on Kamari's behalf.

'It appears that he has lost his voice, father. The grief and trauma surrounding his parents' death may have caused it, however it should return given time.' Kamari noticed that Mauru seemed edgy. Perhaps it was because Lord Hanare had not asked him to sit up yet.

'That is a shame,' he said lightly. 'I was going to ask him if he had any news from the north. I've been receiving some reports that I would like to look into.'

'What kind of reports?' Mauru asked cautiously.

'Nothing important really, I don't think. Oh, you may sit up, boy.' Kamari sat up and sneaked a look around him.

The room was lavishly furnished, the centre dominated by a beautiful maple wood table, surrounded by many cushions for guests to sit on. Lord Hanare was seated on a pile of cushions at the far end of the table, a tea set laid out before him.

Mauru opened his mouth to reply but as he did so the door slid open and the servant entered on his knees, announcing that a messenger had arrived with a report.

'Come in, quickly, quickly,' Hanare said irritably. The messenger entered speedily through the door and bowed low to the floor. 'Stand up and make your report,' he continued.

The messenger stood but kept his eyes averted from the Lord. His tone was anxious, scared even, as he swiftly relayed his message.

'My lord, one of your patrols has just returned from the mountain pass at the end of their sweep. My lord, they... they were attacked, one of the soldiers was killed, they say that a large force is headed this way across the mountains!'

For Kamari, the rest of the messenger's speech seemed to fade away until he could no longer hear what he was saying. His heart was pounding frantically as the jumbled memories prior to his family's flight across the mountains began to rearrange themselves in his mind.

He remembered that his Father had told him it was too dangerous to cross the mountains as they were likely to be trapped by snow, so they had postponed their journey home for another day. That had been the day he had written the letter to Takashi. They had been forced to stay on at his aunt and uncle's house in Morikai Village and Kamari had begun to feel restless.

During the night he had gone outside for some fresh air. This was a welcome break from the stifling heat emanating from the brazier inside the house. He had been sitting on the veranda, staring out into space, when a faint noise had brought him out of his reverie. The noise grew to a deep, bass rumble and then the earth began to quake beneath him. He had stood up and looked northwards along the mountain valley in which the village was situated, but could see only darkness. It was then that the sky had lit up above him.

A sound like that of passing hornets had filled the air as flaming arrows zipped down from the valley sides, crashing through the flimsy thatched roofs and setting them ablaze. Kamari had watched terrified as tongues of flame licked greedily at his uncle's house, wreathing it in a halo of fire. He had rushed inside and yelled at his parents to leave, watching as the roof began to fall in around them. They ran to his aunt and uncle's room but as they got there they heard the splintering of wood and flaming debris rained down upon their sleeping forms.

Terror-stricken, they had sped from the house and, as they did, they spotted the first of the dark figures appearing at the far end of the village. These horrific, shadowy forms advanced with a horrifying intensity, cutting down the helpless villagers as they ran screaming from their burning houses. Their attack had been brutal and merciless, and neither young nor old had been spared.

In an attempt to protect his family, Kamari's father had ordered them to follow him across the mountain, where they at least had a chance at survival.

Something must have shown on his face as he relived these events because Mauru was looking at Kamari intently and when he spoke his voice was quiet but insistent.

'Kamari, do you know about this? Is that what drove your family across the mountains in bad weather?' Kamari nodded slowly, desperately trying to keep his emotions in check in front of Lord Hanare.

'What shall we do?' Mauru said gravely, turning back to his father.

'Do?' Hanare answered mildly. 'We shall do nothing. No upstart army would dare attack an outpost of Harakima. They know too well what Lord Orran's Kurai warriors are capable of and you know as well as I how often that knowledge alone has acted as a deterrent.'

'Well, this feels… different,' Mauru answered slowly. 'This army is moving here from the North; they may have no knowledge of Lord Orran and what he is capable of.'

'Nonsense, Orran is known throughout all five domains of this land. Trust me, they will know of him.'

'Well, if you won't even consider an evacuation, the least you could do is mount a stronger guard on the walls and send out a messenger to Lord Orran,' Mauru answered, a note of anger in his voice.

'You worry too much Mauru,' Hanare replied lightly, 'but I will do as you advise. However, by the morrow you will see that I am right in this.'

'Kamari!' Mauru said in shock. Kamari was trembling violently, his face screwed up in an effort to contain his emotions. 'I must take him home, he may still be suffering from the fever,' Mauru continued quickly.

'Do with him what you will,' Hanare said offhandedly. 'I was going to ask him some more questions but I see that that is impossible. You may leave… oh, and ask the servant to refresh my tea, this pot has gone cold.' Mauru put his arm around Kamari's shoulders and led him from the tea room and out of the building.

'Stubborn fool,' Mauru growled angrily. 'His complacency will get people killed.'

Night was falling over the land, painting long shadows across the earth with a skilled and dexterous hand. The chill evening air seemed to revive Kamari and his shivering lessened as Mauru walked him back to his home. Along the way they passed an armoured warrior on his way to the wall top and Mauru stopped him and whispered quietly into his ear.

'My father is placing an extra wall guard on duty this evening. See to it that the number of men he assigns is doubled.'

'Yes, my lord,' the man replied with a swift bow.

Not long after, Kamari lay again on his straw mat in the darkness, the ghostly orb of the moon visible through the open window. A wolf howled somewhere in the distance and he shivered. Sleep was not easy in coming tonight. As the memories of the past few days swirled in his mind, he was unsure if he would ever sleep peacefully again.

After many hours alone in the dark he felt that he must have fallen asleep and be dreaming for he heard a growing rumble, like that of thunder, and he felt the earth begin to tremble beneath him. A terrified shout rang out from the wall tops outside and Kamari sat bolt upright. At that moment Mauru burst into the room, his breathing fast and harsh. In his hand he held a long, curved sword, a second hanging from his side, and behind him Kamari could see the figures of his wife and daughters.

'Come Kamari, quickly!' he said breathlessly. 'It's just as I thought; we must leave this place, now!'

Kamari leapt up and followed Mauru and his family out through the sliding doors and on to the veranda.

'Take this,' Mauru said, hastily handing Kamari a short sword. 'I must get my father.' Looking out across the village Kamari watched as the villagers left their homes to discover the source of the commotion; watched as the panic began to spread among them like wildfire. Amidst the growing chaos, Kamari spotted Lord Hanare crossing the open ground towards them, surrounded by an armed guard. Before Maura could hurry off Kamari pointed him out and with a fleeting look of relief, Mauru led them out into the open to meet him.

'Of all the brazen impudence!' Lord Hanare yelled above the noise. 'How dare an army march upon Kirina!'

The rumbling abruptly stopped and silence fell over the village, each man and woman now listening intently. A sound could be heard emanating from beyond the northern wall, growing rapidly in volume until all the villagers were quaking in fear.

Clack! Clack! Clack!

As suddenly as it had started, the sound stopped and soon a new sound filled the air above the village.

'Everybody get down, quick!' Kamari yelled, as arrows poured out of the sky, tearing into the earth all around them.

CHAPTER FOUR

A pair of bats flitted through the reddening sky like scraps of fabric caught in the wind, blown here and there on a whim. Sparks burst suddenly into life in the encroaching night as a torch was lit, its ruddy glow casting dancing shadows across the scene. The celebrations for the anniversary had officially begun but it could not have been more overshadowed by anger and rebellion. In an outright display of defiance every family in the village, except the Nariaka and Takami families, had refused to participate, remaining in their homes and not even offering a prayer of thanks to my ancestors.

We had just left the shrine where we had been praying to the Valley Spirit and offering thanks to my ancestors for the lives they had given us. At this point in proceedings it was customary to light a large bonfire and by its light, short plays and comic scenes would be acted out. But, in this social climate, we decided to only light the bonfire. The bonfire itself acts as a strong symbol of life and death, pleasing to the many gods and spirits who roam our land.

When the bonfire had dwindled to embers, we each said a silent prayer then stood up and crossed the bridge back to the west bank.

It was a despondent group of people who were now seated around the low table in my parents' house, their tea sitting forgotten in front of them.

'Their behaviour is totally disrespectful and completely dishonourable,' muttered Yaram Takami, father of the Takami family. 'They show no gratitude for the life your family has given them,' he added, turning to my father.

'They believe we have not done enough to ensure a good harvest this year,' my father replied in a subdued tone.

'If the harvest is bad it is because the gods are punishing them for some misdeed, it is no fault on your part,' Takeda Nariaka put in spiritedly.

'It is not just the harvest... I fear it is more than that,' my father continued, glancing solemnly around. 'They no longer hold any respect for us. Indeed, why should they? What have we done to earn it?'

'Your ancestors rid the land of the southern armies and built this village from the ground up!' Yaram said heatedly. 'They owe you their allegiance!'

'Yes, but what does that mean in this day and age?' my father answered. 'These people are not interested in deeds of the past, they care only about the present, about what is happening now.'

'Then perhaps they should take their own lives in shame!' Yaram said, his voice rising angrily.

Throughout all this I sat in silence, my mind wrapped up in my own anxieties. I was beginning to feel uneasy. I had thought Kamari would have arrived home by now, bursting with stories about his journey across the mountains, but so far there had been no sign of him. I knew his letter had said he might not make it in time, but it felt so wrong without him here. Our need for solidarity was great and without him and his family, the anniversary felt all the more hollow.

The figures seated around the table looked strangely warped and distorted and I found it hard to focus on any of them. I rubbed my eyes, which were aching with tiredness, and noticed that the indistinct shape of my mother was looking at me across the table. I often noticed her looking at me like this, snatching glances when she thought I wasn't aware. I think she pitied me in some way. I think it must have been hard on her to watch me walking around in my eternal sleepless state, knowing that she can do nothing to help me.

I couldn't stay here. The room was stiflingly hot and I wanted to go outside and stretch my legs to fend off my tiredness. I asked my father if I could be excused and he gave me his permission. I bowed formally to the gathering and left as quietly as possible.

A light southerly wind blew through the valley making a refreshing change to the humid air of the tea room. The moon shone brightly in the darkened sky, casting its pale luminescence over the land, completely overshadowing the many pinprick stars surrounding it. I always enjoyed being outside at night. When day reaches its end, a new painter takes over with a new palette and daubs the world in a different colour, a colour that is more subtle and easier on the eyes. He seems also to place a hand over the mouth of the world, muffling its sound, leaving the earth still and quiet.

I had read that night was the time gods and spirits roam our world, moving across the land under cover of darkness. It was said that they were most active in the first hour after midnight, known as the Spirit Hour. I had always wanted to see a spirit, one that was unaware of me and would go about its business unknowingly. But they never revealed themselves.

I could still hear murmured voices coming from the tea room, so I moved away, seeking quiet and solitude. I walked over to the bridge, which was lit on both rails by torches, and sat down on its edge, dangling my legs over the side. Even from here I could feel the villagers' hostility like a wave of hot air. From my vantage point I could see into one house where a husband was shouting angrily at his wife, gesturing in the direction of my home. In another house a man spotted me watching through the window and swiftly blew out his candle, plunging the room into darkness. The furious desperation of his expression lingered in my mind as I sat looking down into the darkened surface of the water below. More than ever before I felt the urge to the leave the village; leave behind all the hatred aimed at me and my family. But this thought made me feel ashamed; I could not leave behind the life that my ancestors had given me.

I stood up slowly and looked northwards along the valley to where the dark outline of the northern mountains bisected the landscape. In my mind's eye I saw Kamari and his parents striding towards me, full of stories to tell. But it was only in my head, and all I could do was wish that they would arrive home soon.

My legs were shaking, my many sleepless nights leaving me feeling weak and insubstantial. I wanted to sleep. I wanted to be able to leave my anxieties behind, at least for a little while, but sleep was as elusive to me as the spirits I so dearly wished to see.

I turned from the bridge and was about to head home for a lie down when a chilling sound made me spin around to face North.

Clack! Clack! Clack!

The sound echoed throughout the valley and fear clutched at my heart. What could be making that terrible noise? Was it some angry spirit? Perhaps a god, come to punish the dissenting villagers?

In every house, candles were lit in windows, splashing pools of orange across the darkened ground as frightened people came to their doors to listen. Looking back at my home I saw my father, Takeda and Yaram, hurrying towards me.

'Takashi, what is going on?' my father asked as he stepped on to the bridge.

'I don't know, father,' I answered worriedly. For a moment the four of us just stood there on the bridge, listening as the unmistakeable sound of marching feet slowly filled the air.

Turning to Takeda, my father spoke in an undertone, 'Alert the villagers. Tell them not to panic and to arm themselves quickly and quietly.' With a swift bow Takeda departed, crossing the bridge and heading into the village. 'Yaram,' my father said, addressing him now. 'Go to my house and warn our families, tell them to stay hidden then collect weapons and bring them back here, hurry!' With a respectful bow, Yaram sped away toward my home, his expression fierce and determined. My Father wore a grim look and put his arm around my shoulders as we looked out to where the sound of marching feet was rapidly growing in volume.

It was not long before Yaram returned bearing weapons and the news that our families were safely hidden back home. We each took a sword. I had trained with weapons throughout my childhood, a skill every child in the village was taught, but I did not pretend that I was as good a fighter as my father at my age, or even Kamari. I remembered the many mornings I had sat and watched Kamari train with a blade or a spear and would often join him as a sparring partner, but he would always beat me.

The swords themselves were lightweight, single-handed things with long, curving blades. Simple and functional, they bore none of the intricate designs and symbols that had adorned the weapons of old; a time when swords were named and their wielders the stuff of legend. I found it funny that I was noticing such small things in the face of an approaching army, for what else could it be? Perhaps it was my way of coping with fear.

We could see them now. They came out of the shadow at the far end of the valley like a dark tide sweeping across the land. Amongst their number I could see many bowmen but thankfully they were not notching arrows to bowstrings. As we watched, we noticed Takeda running toward us from the village. He was breathing heavily by the time he arrived and relayed his message that the villagers were prepared.

'I do not think they will fight,' Takeda said angrily.

'They may yet surprise us when faced with death or enslavement,' my father answered.

The army had reached the village and by the light of their flaming torches their features became clearer and more distinct. Most of the villagers had come outside and I could see that many of them were armed. But next to none of them possessed any real weapons and so had armed themselves with whatever they could. Hoes, picks and other farming implements were now clutched in their shaking hands.

In times past these villagers would have laid down their lives for our families, maintaining their honour and proving their true bravery and loyalty to us. But those times now seemed an eternity away. In the face of this vast and well-armed force their hearts quailed within them. I had doubted they would fight to honour our families but I at least thought they would fight to protect their own. But I was so very wrong. In unison, as though they had never planned to fight, the villagers dropped their weapons like cowards and, turning, shot malicious, hateful glances at my father, whose face never wavered from its steely resolve. I felt tremendous respect for him at that moment; that he should remain calm in the face of this advancing army, when all hope of fending them off was now lost.

As they passed through the village, soldiers peeled off and entered each house, securing the inhabitants one by one, the men putting up no resistance whatsoever.

They were drawing close to the bridge, headed by a man who must have been almost twice my height. On his head he wore a helmet with a single large spike at its top, on to which was thrust a human skull. As he stepped into the light of the bridge, his face was revealed and I saw that it was warped and twisted, almost otherworldly, giving the man a hellish visage.

'They are outsiders,' my father said in disbelief. 'They are not from this land!' The man stopped ten paces from us and raised a hand, pointing imperiously at my father, 'Dar barrak daish!' he hissed. Takeda and Yaram stepped in front of my father and I, their weapons raised.

'Heetu,' the man spat viciously, taking a step backwards.

What happened next appears now only as a blur in my memory. The speed at which it happened and the shock of its occurrence have left little behind that I can recall. From behind the huge man, three soldiers rushed forth wielding large, machete-like weapons. I think Takeda managed to kill one of them with a quick upwards thrust before he and Yaram were mercilessly killed. One of the most vivid things I can recall are the colours. I remember seeing a spray of someone's blood, arcing before my eyes to spatter crimson across the torch-lit wooden boards of the bridge. It is an image that has stayed with me to this day.

Yaram and Takeda crumpled to the floor, their bodies facing the enemy like the true warriors they were, their swords clattering loudly as they hit the wood. The tall man's mouth curled in a malicious grin as he sneered at my father and I. More soldiers began prowling across the bridge towards us, twirling their weapons menacingly. As they drew close to us, my father stepped into their path, shielding me from them.

'Karan mar!' the tall man growled in a low voice. I feel ashamed now when I say that I could not move at that moment. It haunts me still when I close my eyes, but at that time I was young and scared. I watched as though petrified as three soldiers formed a half circle around my Father and began hacking at him with their blades. It was like one of those dreams where you cannot move, even though you are driven by fear and desperation to act. You can see what is happening yet can do nothing about it. You cry out tearfully, desperate to help in some way but your feet are like stones and you stay rooted to the spot and all you can do is watch.

I looked on as his blood pooled in the flickering torch light and dripped off the bridge into the dark water below; watched as the soldiers licked their blades clean, their eyes never leaving mine. It was then that anger and grief overrode the fear and shock that had paralysed me. Snarling like a wolf I hurled myself at the nearest soldier and cut him down before he could move. My blade was hungry for more blood and it slaked its thirst in the belly of the second soldier who could not react fast enough to prevent it. But the third soldier was ready for me and parried my first slash at him. The next thing I felt was searing pain. He had countered with a low slash, opening a gaping wound in my right foot which swiftly welled up with blood. Driven by pain and fury I managed to slice open his stomach horizontally, sending him reeling backwards, but I had forgotten to mind my surroundings. I did not notice the large man stepping towards me until he was almost at my side. His huge hand wrapped around the third soldier's head and flung him into his comrades as he advanced upon me.

Fear drove my hand and I caught him by surprise, my blade finding his thigh beneath his armour and cutting it open. He did not cry out, he did not even flinch, but he reacted with a speed I would not have thought possible of a mortal man. His massive fist, locked around his sword handle, collided with the side of my head. The power of the blow sent me over the railing and into the swift current of the icy water below.

Darkness shrouded my senses and the last thing I remember before blacking-out completely was the sudden agonising pain of an arrow thudding into my side.

CHAPTER FIVE

The first volley of arrows had passed and in that brief pause Kamari, Mauru and his family were able to find cover behind a nearby building. Lord Hanare however, was not so lucky. Three of his guards lay dead on the grass, transfixed by arrows, and the fourth was badly wounded, a shaft protruding from his thigh. He lay writhing on the ground but, courageously, did not cry out in pain. Lord Hanare himself was sprawled on the grass, breathing raggedly, an arrow buried deep in his chest. Blood was oozing from the wound, staining his kimono.

'Stay here,' Mauru said to Kamari and his family. 'I must help my father!' Recklessly, Mauru ran across the open ground to his father and began pulling him towards the cover of the building.

'They may fire a… second volley… leave me,' Hanare gasped painfully. He pulled Mauru towards him and whispered something in his ear. Slowly, Mauru's expression became one of anger and hopelessness.

The hiss of arrows split the air above them as Mauru desperately tried to pull the arrow from his father's chest. 'The shaft is barbed, please go… now!'

Hanare roared the last word at his son. With one last look at him, Mauru turned and ran back towards his family. Arrows began to sprout from the ground all around him and as he reached the cover of the building a shaft tore through his right forearm.

Mauru slumped down against the building and gritted his teeth as a wave of pain washed over him. His wife crawled to his side and looked into his face tearfully. Taking his arm gently in her lap she snapped the arrow in two and carefully withdrew it, then pulled him close and hugged him tight.

'What are we going to do?' Kamari asked anxiously.

'We have to leave Kirina,' Mauru answered, wincing as his wife bound the wound with a strip of cloth from her kimono. He stood, his face ashen, and cautiously made his way to the other end of the building. From this position he had a good view of the northern edge of the village where the arrows had come from. Kamari moved up behind Mauru and looked out northwards with him. In the light of the torches ranged along the walls, armoured warriors could be seen scaling the wall on top of ladders and jumping to the platform below. Many Kirina soldiers lay slain along the platform, barbed shafts sticking from their throats.

'The stables,' Mauru said quickly to Kamari. 'If we can get horses, we may be able to escape. Everyone, quietly follow me.' Mauru led Kamari, his wife and his daughters, who had remained bravely silent throughout the ordeal, out into the open ground between the buildings, heading towards the dark shape of the stables. As they moved, the shadowy figures of the invading army began circling the buildings not far ahead, drawing ever closer to them. Shouts and screams could be heard echoing from all around as the unprepared villagers were captured or killed by the merciless horde.

Buildings had begun to blaze along the northern edge of the village as the army swept southwards between the houses. Dark, searing red gave way to amber and yellow in the roaring flames that pitilessly ravaged the simple homes, sending ash, sparks and smoke high into the still night air.

As Mauru drew close to the open door of the stables he was forced to leap aside as a panic-stricken horse galloped towards him, blood flowing from a wound on its haunches. More horses followed but Mauru was unable to catch the beasts, which fled terrified into the night.

'Wait out here,' Mauru said firmly to Kamari and his family. 'I'm going to have a look inside.' Drawing his sword Mauru entered the stable.

Three soldiers stood by the body of a horse lying spread-eagled on the floor. Their weapons were drawn, the blades stained with blood. They had been releasing and killing the horses indiscriminately, making sure that no one would be able to escape on them. They turned as Mauru entered and looked at each other, their grotesque faces creasing into gleeful grins, and slowly began to advance on him.

The stable was dimly lit by a sputtering oil lantern hanging from the cross beams of the ceiling. By its light Mauru could see that they were approaching with an air of complacence that he could use to his advantage. They clearly believed he would be no match for them. They began to circle him, licking their blades in anticipation of the slaughter to come. As they closed in tighter around him Mauru feinted to his right and expertly dispatched the soldier to his left, his blade finding the man's throat and nearly rending his head from his shoulders. The soldier to his right lowered his guard momentarily, watching dumbstruck as the body of his comrade collapsed to the floor, gushing blood. This small lapse in concentration was all Mauru needed to disarm the man and open a large diagonal wound across his flimsily armoured chest, watching coldly as he fell to the floor, gurgling softly.

The sickening hiss of a blade passing through flesh was the only sound Mauru heard in the silence after the second man's passing. He turned slowly and saw the third soldier standing close behind him, his weapon poised. Blood blossomed from the soldier's chest as he looked down in shock at the sword point protruding from his torso. The blade withdrew with a metallic sucking noise, leaving the soldier to fall limply to the floor. Kamari stood in the stable doorway; a blood-stained short sword clutched in his trembling hand. He let it fall to the ground, staring at the body, a mixture of shock and disbelief on his face. He sat down shakily; his eyes still trained on the man he had killed. The blood had drained from Kamari's face and he appeared almost wraithlike in the weak light.

Mauru bowed to Kamari in thanks then strode over to him, grasping him by the shoulders and helping him to his feet.

'There will be time for that later,' Mauru said roughly. 'We will all have many things to grieve for, but right now we must leave.' A nervous whinny to their left made Mauru spin around. His horse Dagri was still tied in his stable, apparently unharmed but looking very frightened. His eyes were rolling in their sockets and he was stamping the ground fearfully.

With an anxious look back at the stable entrance, Mauru strode towards Dagri and began untying him, whispering softly and stroking his nose to calm him. He led the horse over to the equipment rack and saddled him up, then put his arm round Kamari's shoulder and they left the stables together.

As soon as he got outside, Sen, Chiro and Akayama huddled close to Mauru, hugging him tightly, tears pouring silently down their faces.

'We had feared the worst,' Sen said quietly, looking at her husband. He kissed her softly and hugged his daughters while Kamari stood nervously to one side, feeling awkward.

'They haven't spotted us yet,' Mauru whispered. 'We must get to the main gate and leave Kirina now, while we still have a chance.'

Crossing the darkened land to the gateway was a harrowing experience for all of them. Every rustle in the shadows became the advancing steps of an enemy warrior, every breath of wind was an arrow rushing to meet them. After what seemed like many hours, they made it to the gate and, working together, managed to push the large crossbar from the hooks and inch the door carefully open.

Once outside Kamari sat heavily on the ground, breathing quickly. He had realised for the first time, with a chilling wave of horror, that this army was unlikely to stop at Kirina and the next obvious target was, 'Aigano!' he breathed fearfully. 'I must get home and warn Takashi!' Mauru turned to Kamari, his expression grim but determined.

'You should take Dagri,' he said forcefully. 'My father...' He stopped and sounded like he found it hard to go on. 'He did not warn Lord Orran as I requested.'

'What!' Kamari spluttered. 'Why did he not listen to...?'

'Take Dagri and ride to Harakima, warn all there of this threat!' Mauru cut across him.

'But what about you... your family?' Kamari answered desperately.

'Use your sense!' Mauru retorted hotly, tears forming in his eyes. 'We could not all fit on one horse! I will look after my family; I want you to go, now!' Trembling with emotion Kamari bowed to Mauru, his tears falling to the damp grass. Swiftly he clambered into Dagri's saddle and looked back.

'I believe the gods are smiling on you,' Mauru said fondly, handing him one of the two long bladed swords hanging from his side. Arrows began to hit the earth all around them as the invading army stormed through the village towards the open gates. In fright Dagri bolted and Kamari did not have a chance to say goodbye as he was carried off into the night. The last thing Kamari saw of them was their small, dark shapes heading quickly southwest towards a nearby forest as soldiers began to pour through the open gates.

Kirina had receded to a dull red glow in the distance as Dagri galloped madly onwards. Kamari was terrified. The horse paid no heed to his efforts to slow him down, pounding wildly on in the darkness, snorting in fright. Kamari feared that he would be thrown from the saddle and crushed but, somehow, he managed to cling on throughout his wild ride. He needed to bring the horse under control for he had no idea if they were going in the right direction. He had to get back to Aigano and warn all there. For all he knew the army could be marching toward his home right now.

Hours passed as dawn steadily broke across the horizon, infusing the sky with red and gold hues, yet Dagri showed no signs of stopping. His sides were heaving with exertion and it became clear that if he did not stop soon he would collapse. As the sun rose higher, Dagri steadily slowed his pace until Kamari felt it was safe to jump from the saddle. As he did so the horse stopped completely and with an exhausted snort collapsed onto his side, missing Kamari by inches.

In the pale light of day, the surrounding landscape was revealed to Kamari. Hot tears of frustration poured down his face as he realised that during the night they had ridden way off course, far into the west. Despair and shame descended upon him as he lay on the damp grass. Aigano could come under attack within hours and he could have warned them. He wept bitterly, curling into a ball as all hope left him.

Dagri's breathing had calmed and he had begun to eat some of the nearby grass. Kamari lay on his side watching the horse and soon his resolve began to return. Dagri seemed to have overcome his fear. Perhaps now it would be safe to ride him again…

Rising slowly, Kamari walked over to him and stroked him soothingly, grasping his reins and gently pulling the horse to his feet. He spoke to him quietly and reassuringly as he began to lead him southeast in the direction of Aigano. *There is still a chance*, Kamari kept telling himself over and over as he led the horse onwards, waiting for his strength to return so he could ride him, *there is still a chance…*

By midday Dagri seemed strong enough to bear Kamari's weight. Climbing swiftly into the saddle he urged the horse onwards but no matter how hard he tried he could not encourage Dagri into a gallop. He had to make up lost ground, but Dagri would go no faster than a trot.

On they went for hours with Kamari becoming more and more frustrated until at last Dagri broke into a controllable gallop and Kamari finally felt they could catch up. But the time spent allowing Dagri to recover had paid its price and already night was setting in. The moon had begun its steady rise to replace the sun and the daytime sounds of birds and insects soon dwindled and ceased. Kamari knew he was very close but as night fell completely he decided it would be best to stop and rest, rather than risk getting lost again in the dark.

He continued on for as long as he could but was soon forced to stop as he could no longer see what was in front of him. They had come to a halt near a small wooded area and he decided they would rest there for a few hours. He tied Dagri to a young cedar and then sat down with his back against the trunk. He wished for the comforting warmth of a fire but knew it would be unwise to advertise their presence and he had neither flint nor tinder anyway. To his left, Dagri settled down in the grass and was soon asleep. It was only then that Kamari realised how tired he was. He had only managed a few hours' sleep the previous night before Mauru had woken him.

Thinking about Mauru, he began to wonder, what must have happened to them? Were he and his family alright? Had they been captured? Or were they even now in the hands of those hideous barbarians? The questions swirled in his brain but he knew he could not think about them now. He needed to get a few hours' sleep, ready for the last stretch homewards in the morning. Would he be too late? This was the one thing he could think of as he fell into a fitful slumber.

He awoke several hours later and realised that fortunately day had only just broken. He had been having nightmares of oversleeping and not reaching Aigano in time. Dagri was happily crunching grass and seemed ready for another fast ride. Within minutes they were underway and in daylight Kamari could see just how close he had come the previous night when visibility had been poor. Kohaku Valley was not far away and Kamari realised that they would be there within the hour.

As he drew closer and closer to his home his skin began to crawl and a feeling of dread pervaded his entire body. He had reached the northern end of the valley, where the small rolling hills gradually grew into the steep valley sides further south, but not a sound could be heard anywhere. The air would usually have been filled with voices and the sounds of people at work in the fields, but an unnatural quiet seemed to have descended upon the valley.

He leapt down from Dagri and led him to the top of a low rise where he was afforded his first real view of Aigano. He fell to his knees in shock.

'No…' he whispered.

Black smoke billowed up from the ruins of the houses. Dead animals and other debris littered the ground and the village appeared deserted. He was too late. During the night, while he had stopped to rest, the army had attacked Aigano, enslaving or murdering anyone they found.

He had not reached home in time. He had failed them.

CHAPTER SIX

The first thing I became aware of was the sun's heat beating down on my face, my vision crimsoned through my closed eyelids. My head throbbed excruciatingly, sending dull pain lancing throughout my whole body. My clothes felt damp to the touch, as though I had been submerged bodily in water, and sure enough, not far away, I could hear the gurgle of a river. My foot felt as though it was on fire and it was then that I sensed someone nearby. A hand touched my foot and I recoiled, scrabbling blindly backwards in the grass.

'Takashi!'

I stopped. I knew that voice. He had been my loyal friend for as long as I could remember and somehow, against the odds, he was now kneeling right by my side.

'Kamari?' I whispered in disbelief. I tried to open my eyes but the glare of the sun only increased the pain in my head.

'Sit still,' Kamari said quietly. 'I'll bind the wound on your foot.' I heard the sound of fabric tearing and then felt pressure being applied to my foot as he bound it tightly with a strip of cloth.

'My side,' I said weakly, my hand gingerly touching the wound.

'I pulled the arrow out and bandaged it,' Kamari answered. 'It was just a flesh wound; it will heal quickly.' The horrific memories of last night's events collided with the many questions I wanted to ask Kamari and for a moment I did not know where to begin.

'Your parents,' I began feebly. 'Where are they? What happened to you…? I thought that maybe you'd…'

'I couldn't help them,' he said and I detected a note of shame in his voice. 'I couldn't help anyone.'

'What do you mean? What happ…'

'They're dead,' he said shortly, his voice quivering as he spoke. He sighed deeply, and for a moment I thought that he would say no more on the subject. But then, as though he wished to get the story off his chest, he related everything that had happened since he had written me that letter all those days ago. There were many points where I thought he would not be able to continue, but he bravely carried on with his story, his voice choked but gathering strength. Before he finished, he told me that he had found me floating face up in the river. I had been caught in the reeds by the bank, the water reddening around me, and he had dragged me on to solid ground.

When he had finished, I sat in silence, thinking about all the hardships he had been through to get back home. I felt a strong sense of solidarity with him then, stronger than I had ever felt before. I had always thought of him as my brother and right now, that bond was more important than ever.

I was able to look around now, squinting in the dazzling sunlight, my head still thudding painfully.

'They must have got here mere hours before me,' Kamari said in an undertone, his head bowed. 'I could have prevented this. I could have warned everyone.'

'You did all you could,' I replied reassuringly. 'It was not your fault the horse was uncontrollable.' After a long pause Kamari spoke again.

'So... what happened to you? Your family? Are they alright?' I had become so wrapped up in Kamari's story and the hardships he had been through that I had almost forgotten my own troubles. Everything that had happened the previous night came painfully to the fore in my mind and the stark reality of our situation became apparent. Grief overcame me and it was many minutes before I felt able to speak. I was so tired. At that moment in time I would have liked nothing more than to be able to fall asleep, but there was much to be done and after hearing Kamari's story, I knew that time was not on our side.

I tried to stand and Kamari helped me to my feet.

'I need to... I need to check on something,' I said jerkily, my legs wobbling unsteadily beneath me as I started in the direction of the bridge with Kamari supporting me.

Their bodies were still there, cold as stones to the touch, left disrespectfully to the elements. I turned away from them, unable to look any longer as tears flowed freely down my bloodless face. I had been brought up to control my emotions at all times, like a warrior, but I no longer cared for that as images from last night danced mockingly before my eyes. Without a word I crossed the bridge, Kamari following silently behind, and headed towards my home across the dry and brittle grass.

It was a scene of devastation. The wood and paper screens partitioning the different rooms had been torn down and trampled underfoot and all my books and scrolls lay in tattered fragments everywhere. The shrine had been knocked over and cruelly defiled and the air around me smelt of blood and sweat. My family was nowhere to be seen.

I left the house and sat on the step by the door where Kamari had been quietly waiting. I felt strangely disconnected from everything around me as I sat there, trying to comprehend the events that had occurred over the last few hours. In no time at all my life had changed irreversibly and I had no idea why it had happened.

'So, what are we going to do?' Kamari asked after a pause. I felt tremendous gratitude that he did not ask me to explain my story. For me, the grief was far too close, and I would need time and space before I could talk about it. Mutely, I nodded at the bridge, for I found it hard to say what needed to be done, but Kamari understood my meaning.

We buried all three bodies in the small cemetery at the north end of the village, which thankfully had been left untouched by the barbarian army. It was common for bodies to be burnt to ashes before burying them but I did not have the heart to do so. It took all my courage to simply bury them; I could not watch their bodies burn. We had none of the traditional ceremonial items to aid the passing of their spirits, so all that was left to us was to pray for their peaceful journey. We had however managed to scratch their names on stones with a sword point to place on the graves.

We knelt in silence for over an hour, each wrapped up in our own private thoughts, but we both knew that we must move on soon. Reluctantly, I stood and we left the cemetery, bowing low to the floor as a mark of respect before leaving.

'We need to go to Harakima and warn the lord there,' Kamari said as we walked slowly away. 'We cannot allow this to happen to other villages. Do you know the way there?' I winced with each step as we walked south through the village. I was limping badly and began to worry that it might become permanent.

'I know that it's somewhere southeast of here,' I replied, thinking back to all the stories I had read about the famous castle town. 'I don't think it's too far but we'll need food and water if we're going to survive the journey. Feels like I haven't eaten in days.'

We searched the wreckage of the houses and managed to find a sizeable amount of dry rice, enough to keep us going for a week or more; the main problem was having enough water to cook it in. We also found two bowls and some plums and other fruit that were not too badly damaged, so we put them all in the rice sack.

Searching Kamari's house, we found numerous heavy flasks which we filled with water from the river. After much searching, we also came up with flint and tinder, which would be useful for starting fires to boil the rice, and a metal pot to boil it in.

While Kamari went to fetch Dagri from the tree he had tied him to, I returned to the bridge and picked up one of the swords that had been dropped there. I was unsure who it had belonged to but I knew I needed to be protected so I slung it horizontally from the cloth belt around my waist. I picked up the remaining two swords, uncomfortable to just leave them there, and as an afterthought slung a second blade by the first at my side. Before leaving the bridge for the last time I bowed low to the floor and said a silent prayer for those who had fallen there. I stood slowly, my eyes dry, and left the bridge without a backwards glance.

Kamari arrived leading Dagri by his reins. He was indeed a magnificent specimen of a horse, a champion of his kind, although his temperament left much to be desired. He was very shy and at first would not allow me to come near him, let alone touch him, but eventually I won his trust and he allowed me to stroke his muscular neck.

'I suppose I don't blame him really,' Kamari said, stroking Dagri's face pensively. 'We all get scared sometimes.'

'He seems fine now,' I answered. 'I think we'd best make a start.' We slung the heavy water flasks and the metal rice pot over Dagri's saddle, turning him into a kind of packhorse, but he did not seem to mind. I gave the last remaining sword to Kamari before we began our journey southwards. We had to reach the end of the valley before we would be able to cut off south-east and head in the direction of Harakima.

It is hard to describe the emotions I felt upon leaving Kohaku Valley. So many memories crowded my mind, clamouring for attention, that the only thing I can now remember is feeling confused. I thought back to the many sleepless nights I had spent in my family home, imagining that I was off on some journey or adventure like the warriors in the stories of old, but I never thought that it would actually happen to me. I never wanted my own adventure to begin like this.

As we walked through the silent valley, I realised how difficult it was for me to speak to Kamari at this time. I had never had trouble talking to him about anything, but after the events of the past few days we both found it hard to strike up any kind of conversation.

As I could think of nothing to say, I tried to recall as much information about Harakima as I could from the many scrolls I had read on the castle. From what I remembered it was a large, well-fortified castle town, whose sturdy walls protected not just the lord, but his entire army and his people. The lord who ruled the castle was an enormously respected man by the name of Orran, whose ancestors had ruled the Hirono Domain for many generations.

I knew little of how the Orrans actually came to power, other than that at one time the domain had been split into many different provinces and the lords of each province had been locked in a power struggle for control of the whole domain. The Orran line had eventually taken control, abolishing the other lords and their provinces and unifying them into one peaceful domain.

Since the Orrans came to power they had been protected by a renowned army of warriors known as the Kurai. They are a highly disciplined and courageous group who, from birth, devote their lives and their swords entirely to their lord, who commands their complete loyalty and respect. Little else was known about the Kurai and their way of life as they tended to keep to themselves, living in a secluded area of the castle town away from the common villagers.

I returned from my thoughts when I noticed that Kamari was standing stock still and appeared to be listening intently. I stopped by his side and followed his gaze southward to where the valley sides began to shrink into the ground and level out. To our right the Daku River curved off south and slightly west, disappearing into the distance. I could not see anything out of the ordinary.

'What is it?' I whispered. Kamari did not answer straight away. He stood alert, listening for the slightest sound.

'Thought I heard someone,' he eventually answered quietly.

'They may still be around here,' I said, drawing my sword. 'We should leave Dagri here and scout ahead.' Kamari nodded and swiftly tied Dagri to a nearby maple tree on the lower slopes.

We advanced cautiously through the long grass by the river, tense and alert, heading towards a shape up ahead that we both knew well. Many years ago, Aigano village had been much bigger, stretching almost to the end of the valley. A large and, at one time, very beautiful shrine had been built where the entrance to the village once stood. But as times became harder and people left or died, the village had shrunk, and where houses had once been only grass now grew. The only testament that remained to Aigano's former greatness was the ruined shrine, marking the edge of the village. It had been expertly built from chiselled stone and each of its many roofs had been tiled in bamboo canes. Within the shrine, the walls had been covered in many engravings;

likenesses of the Valley Spirit and words of gratitude for good harvests and peaceful years. But the passing of time and many years of negligence had thrown it into disrepair and it stood now as a hollow shell - a symbol of lost faith.

The fact that the army had passed through here was obvious to both of us. The shrine appeared now in worse condition than we had ever seen it. From where we stood we could discern fresh engravings on the mossy, tumbledown stones. Unintelligible, barbaric words sat alongside hideous drawings of brutal slaughter and burning houses and here and there crimson patches of blood stood out starkly against the grey stone. I trembled with fury as I looked upon this wanton pollution of our once great shrine.

Then from out of nowhere, or so it seemed, an arrow tore past my face, grazing my cheek before hitting the soft grass some distance behind us. We dropped swiftly to the ground and looked at each other. My cheek stung painfully and I felt blood oozing from the wound. The arrow had come from the area in front of the shrine, the assailant hidden from view by a pile of fallen stones. We nodded to each other and began to crawl forwards on our bellies, our swords still clutched tightly in our hands.

When we reached the pile of stones, I whispered to Kamari to circle around so that we would catch our attacker from two sides. I waited for him to get as close as possible to our assailant's hiding place before I made my move around the stones. I noticed many pools of blood as I drew near to where I could hear the bowman breathing heavily.

I peeked over the stones and caught my first glimpse of him. He had his back to me as he had just heard a sound made by Kamari directly opposite. Fumblingly he managed to notch an arrow to his bowstring and unsteadily pointed it in the direction of Kamari. I had to make my move now.

Silently I clambered over the stones and crept up behind him. It was as he was drawing the bow back for release that he felt the cold steel of my blade against his throat. Falteringly he released the tension in the bowstring and set his bow and arrow to one side. It was only then that I noticed he was bleeding. Thick red-black blood was seeping from an ugly wound in his stomach.

'Look at me,' I said as recognition began to dawn. I don't know whether he understood me or not but the sound of my voice made him turn his head and look painfully up into my face. I realised then with a sick feeling in my stomach that he was one of the three soldiers who had attacked my Father. The debilitating wound that had caused him to be left behind by his own comrades had been inflicted by me. At that moment Kamari emerged from the ruined shrine, an anxious expression on his face; but he did not approach us. He simply stood quietly and watched.

'Tell me what your army is doing here,' I hissed angrily, 'and I will make your passing quick.' The soldier choked on the blood pouring from his mouth and began to speak quickly in his own tongue, a savage snarl curling his lips.

'Tell me!' I shouted, pressing the blade hard against his throat until it drew blood. I looked down into his pitiless craggy face as he managed to splutter out two words, almost incoherently.

'Orran's… Blade.' With one swift motion I drew the blade sharply across his throat. The soldier made one last dying gurgle before slumping backwards against the ruined stones, his eyes slowly clouding over.

I raised my head and noticed that Kamari was looking at me strangely. He seemed shocked, as though he could not believe what I had just done. But I have no remorse for what I did. None.

We did not think it respectful to leave the body to rot in the Valley Spirit's shrine so Kamari and I dragged it to the river and flung it in, watching dispassionately as the current dragged it away. Without a word, Kamari went to fetch Dagri and our supplies, leaving me to stand alone by the swiftly flowing water. For several minutes I simply stood there and stared down at my distorted reflection.

I often think about the man I killed in cold blood, who died sitting defenceless on the ground. In the end I believe his fate was a result of his actions in life. It is the way of things - for every evil deed committed by a person there will be an inevitable consequence.

Kamari arrived leading Dagri. I noticed that he gave me a sideways look as we started out in a south-easterly direction, but he did not say anything. As we left Kohaku I turned and looked upon the valley, my home, for what may be the last time. I realised then how strange it is that you never realise and truly appreciate the things that you have, until you no longer have them.

CHAPTER SEVEN

An ocean of tall grass stretched out before us, buffeted gently by a light wind, making it appear to ripple like water. The tips of the grass brushed against our thighs as we strode in the direction of Harakima, thankful for the breeze that cooled the heat of the late afternoon sun. It was very quiet; the only sound we could hear was the gentle clinking of the load Dagri bore as we led him onward. We had been walking for many hours but had said very little since we left Kohaku Valley. I began to wonder what Kamari thought of the way I had dealt with that soldier. Had I gone too far? Would Kamari have done the same thing in my place? Would he ever speak to me again? But as the soldier's hideous face swam before my eyes and the bodies on the bridge crowded my senses, I cast these doubts aside.

Several hours passed. Kamari's silence was becoming unbearable and before long I felt I had to say something.

'What do you think he meant by "Orran's Blade"?' I asked quietly. I wanted to say, "You believe I should not have killed him," and discover whether he believed my cold-blooded killing was justified or not, but somehow I could not bring myself to say it.

'I have never heard of such a thing,' Kamari answered slowly, squinting his eyes to peer off into the distance.

'Well, it must belong to Lord Orran,' I said thoughtfully. 'But no army would dare march upon Harakima, the Kurai are too strong. What is so important about Lord Orran's Blade?'

Kamari did not answer. Instead he stopped and raised his arm to point southwards.

'Look at that, Takashi,' he breathed in an awestruck voice. I followed his gaze and looked in the direction he was indicating and the sight I saw left me speechless. I had read about this in many books chronicling the history of our lands, but I never thought I would actually see it. In truth I never even thought I would leave Aigano. The dark outline snaked its way across the horizon to the south, running from the far western shores for many, many miles into the east. Built hundreds of years ago, the immense wall known as "Agrath's Deterrent" was an awesome spectacle. I could not even guess at the number of years it had taken to complete it. It had been built under the rule of Lord Agrath Armani to keep the invading southern hordes from attacking his provinces. The walls were well fortified and many times the height of an average man, protected by numerous guard towers where the Lord's soldiers could keep a wary eye out for threats.

'I did not think man could build anything so big,' Kamari whispered, his eyes locked on the horizon.

'I have read about a similar wall in a land across the seas. It is said to be many times greater in size - thousands of miles long,' I replied, glad that Kamari was now talking more normally to me.

'I would not have believed it if I had not seen it,' he said after a pause.

'From what I've read Harakima castle is grander still, this wall should be nothing in comparison,' I answered with a smile. After a few more moments of quiet staring Kamari looked up at the waning sun and squared his shoulders.

'We should press on,' he said stoically. 'We need to find somewhere to camp before it gets dark and I could do with some food.' I nodded in agreement and we continued on in an easterly direction, headed towards a tree lined hillock that would give a good view of the surrounding landscape.

Night was falling as we neared the tree line, blanketing the world in shadow and fear. Kamari yawned as we drew closer to the trees, his eyes heavy with sleep. I put out an arm to stop him when I saw a shape moving softly in the shadows. The moon was behind a cloud so I could not see clearly what it was but I could hear the rustling of leaves as it shuffled around. It did not appear to be moving far, staying close to an area that I could not see.

Moonlight suddenly spilled across the earth, chasing away the shadows to reveal a full-grown male wolf standing tense and alert outside his den. With a jolt of pity, I noticed that at his feet lay the body of his mate, lying limp and cold on a carpet of fallen leaves. I could not tell what had killed the female wolf but it seemed clear to me that the male had not left her side since she had died. His proud face turned slowly to look at us and his expression held a depth of sorrow I did not think animals were capable of. He threw back his head and howled, baying his pain to the moon. That moment has stuck with me forever after, even to this day after so much has happened.

He dropped his head and glanced at us one more time before wandering off into the forest. As he moved he snuffed at the ground as though searching for something and slowly melted into the darkness between the trees. I could not explain it, not even to myself, but somehow I knew that he would never return to this place.

In our village wolves were sacred animals, beloved by the Valley Spirit, and it was considered an unredeemable crime to cause harm to them in any way. The elders of our village would often say that spirits clung to wolves like shrouds, that they were vessels for the world beyond, but I never fully understood what they meant by that. I had often seen wolves moving between the maples and cedars around our village and I always took the utmost care never to disturb them. I held great respect for their kind and after a quick look at Kamari we bowed to the dead female before moving a respectable distance away to make our camp.

After some difficulty we managed to light a fire with flint and tinder and soon had some rice boiling in the pot Dagri had been carrying. We sat in silence, each running through the events of the previous few days in our minds. As I sat there, I realised this was my first ever night away from my home and my family. For Kamari, this night was not as strange as it was for me, for he had of course been away before when visiting his grandparents across the mountains. However, this night was unsettling for both of us. We were alone in the wilderness, far from home, and far from help.

When the rice was ready we scooped heaped bowlfuls of it and ate with our hands, shovelling it in hungrily as it had been many hours since our last meal. When we had finished, we washed out our bowls and drank from them, quenching the thirst that the day's sun had left us with.

'We should try and get some rest now,' Kamari yawned sleepily, 'we have a long journey ahead of us tomorrow.'

'I won't be able to sleep,' I replied. 'Certainly not after what's happened.' I could feel Kamari looking at me across the fire for many minutes before he next spoke.

'You still see his face?' he asked. I stared into the fire, watching as ash drifted lazily into the night sky.

'Every night,' I answered quietly. In the embers of the dying fire the image of the man who had cut down my grandfather flickered before my eyes and still I had no idea who he was, or what motives had driven him. 'I'll just keep watch for tonight... I've got a lot to think about.'

Kamari stared at me a moment longer before he bade me goodnight and turned onto his side with his back to the fire. Before long his light breathing signified he had fallen asleep. I drew my knees up under my chin and sat for many minutes listening to the night-time noises of the forest around me. The wind whistled softly through the tree tops above and I could hear the sounds of birds settling down to roost.

When I was sure Kamari was sound asleep, I stole quietly away, curled up at the base of a tree nearby and I wept. I wept for my family, wherever they were now. I wept for my father; whose guiding hand had now slipped from my own. I wept from loss and hardship and emptiness. And I wept because I was so tired that I almost could not see, but still I could not fall asleep.

I watched dispiritedly through the trees as dawn broke hazily across the horizon, picking out the dark, uneven outline of Agrath's Deterrent against the pale sky. I sat with my back against the tree for many hours as Kamari slumbered on, watching the world awaken around me through puffy, swollen eyes. My imagination played out scenes before me and I saw the things Kamari had gone through to get back to Aigano as though I had been there with him. Then, unbidden, I saw again the night my village was attacked and though I tried to dispel the images, I found that I could not.

Kamari woke with a start beside the smouldering fire and looked around groggily.

'Did you say something?' he said, snapping me back to reality and rescuing me from reliving that night.

'No, I don't think so,' I answered as I sat up and stretched.

'Huh, sounded like you were calling out,' Kamari mumbled as he reached for a stick to stoke the fire.

For the morning meal we ate some more rice and a couple of the plums that were only slightly bruised. We allowed Dagri to drink some of our water from the pot we boiled rice in before we set off again in the direction we believed Harakima stood.

Kamari seemed much more cheerful after a good night's sleep and we spent the morning talking amicably as we walked through long grass with the sun rising high in the east. It occurred to me that maybe Kamari had heard me crying last night and had resolved to cheer me up, but if he had he said nothing of it.

I found Kamari's bravery inspiring. After everything he'd been through he was still the same as I remembered him; still able to make me laugh and bring me out of myself. I needed someone like him right then. If he had not been there I probably would not have got up from the base of the tree where I spent the night and would have remained trapped there by my own imagination.

I think Kamari began to worry about me around early afternoon. I had noticed him casting anxious looks in my direction while trying to maintain a happy demeanour, so when he called a stop after saying he was hungry I knew he just wanted me to have a rest. We stopped by a small stream that ran through a grove of cedar trees and when I lowered my head to splash water on my face I noticed how pale my complexion was and saw the dark rings around my bloodshot eyes.

I had thought washing my face in cold water would help wake me up but all it did was leave me with a numb headache.

'If you want to try and get some rest I'll keep watch for a while,' Kamari said as I stumbled back towards him from the stream. I was so tired I could only grunt in agreement. I kicked off my sandals and threw myself down on the soft grass, shutting my eyes to welcome darkness.

I awoke a couple of hours later to find Kamari shaking me by the shoulder. I had finally managed to get a few minutes of sleep, but most of the time had been spent lying in an almost paralysed state, somewhere between sleeping and waking. But I felt better for the time I had managed to sleep, even though my dreams had been chaotic and terrifying.

'We should probably be moving on now,' he said gently, still with an anxious look on his face. 'If you're ready that is? We need to cover as much ground as we can before nightfall.'

'Alright,' I answered resignedly. 'I feel better now. I think I'm ready to go.'

We had been walking for a few hours and the day was drawing to its end. The sky was a deep blue and the rising moon stood out vividly against this brilliant backdrop.

Although Kamari did not say it, I believe he was thinking it. I was slowing him down, and after what he had witnessed at Kirina I knew he wanted to reach Harakima as fast as possible and warn everyone there. I tried my hardest to keep up with his lengthy strides, but every few steps my eyelids would close and I would stumble. It felt like walking through deep water or sand and try as I might, I could not force myself to walk any faster.

I don't think he was angry with me in any way, just frustrated perhaps. He was never disrespectful and continued to make cheery conversation throughout the journey, which helped to stave off my tiredness a little.

As we walked, I had the strange feeling we were being watched. It began as a shiver that ran through my body and raised the hairs on the nape of my neck, leaving me with the nagging feeling that eyes were upon us. I looked around warily through half-closed eyes and noticed something in a grove of trees to the north.

Now, when I think back to that time, I cannot be certain that my mind was not playing tricks on me. What I believe I saw, whether it was real or imaginary, was almost beyond description. In the depths of the trees I saw a light that illuminated the surrounding area for some distance. Then a creature, for that is the only word I can think of to describe it, stepped out from behind a tree and stood for a moment, looking in my direction.

At first glance it looked like a man, but he was much taller than a normal man and appeared to be dressed in light. But as I looked closer, he seemed also to take on the appearance of a massive wolf with a thick mane of dark hair.

My immediate thought was that I had at last seen a spirit, but when I turned to Kamari and tugged his kimono, it had vanished, before either of us could have another look at it.

I apologised and told him I had merely seen another wolf in the trees. I did not want to confess at that time that perhaps my imagination was running away with me. But although I cannot be sure what I saw that evening was real, I like to think that it was in fact my first ever sighting of a true spirit.

It was drawing close to the Spirit Hour and we still had not found a suitable place to spend the night. It was now so dark we could not even see our hands in front of our faces. We were both aching with tiredness; even Dagri could barely lift his hooves as we trudged onwards. As we walked, we looked everywhere for somewhere to rest and shelter from the wind - a forest, the overhang of a hill, anything - but none were forthcoming.

By this point we were so exhausted that we could scarcely raise our heads. Walking slowly, I glanced upwards and noticed with surprise what looked like blurred balls of fire, floating in the air. Kamari had his head bowed wearily and had not spotted them.

'Look at that,' I said, nudging him. 'What do you think they are?' With an effort Kamari looked up and his brow creased in confusion.

'I don't know, maybe it's...' his expression changed to one of relief and happiness. 'They're torches! It must be some kind of building. Maybe we've finally found Harakima!' he yelled excitedly.

We both broke into a run and sped towards the torches as the outline of a building became apparent in the weak moonlight.

CHAPTER EIGHT

A shaft of moonlight picked out the main gate but in the darkness it was hard to tell how big the building was. I was certain, however, that this could not be Harakima. Breathing heavily, we drew up to the iron-studded main gates, which were lit on either side by torches.

'Hey!' Kamari yelled up at a sentry standing alert upon the wall top. 'We have travelled for days to get here, is this Harakima Castle, seat of Lord Orran?' The sentry had an arrow pulled taut on his bowstring and was aiming agitatedly at Kamari.

'I'll ask the questions,' the sentry barked. 'What brings you here at this hour?'

'We have an urgent message for Lord Orran!' Kamari shouted back. 'We must speak with him, immediately!'

'Well you have come to the wrong place,' he answered, lowering his bow. 'This is Toramo Village. Harakima is a day's walk east of here, now be about your business!' The guard turned to walk away along the wall but I stopped him.

'Wait! We have a warning; we need to speak to your lord, it is of great importance!'

'If you want lords you should continue on to Harakima, we have none here,' he replied, turning slowly. 'We are not ruled by one man.' Kamari threw caution to the winds and decided to tell this sentry what had happened.

'There is an army come out of the north,' he said loudly. 'They are murderers... barbarians... They have already killed or enslaved hundreds. If they have not attacked here then they must have headed back north but I do not doubt they will be on your doorstep soon.'

It was some time before the sentry seemed able to form a reply to this startling news.

'This is true?' the man asked quietly.

'It is,' we both replied. The sentry turned and yelled to someone we could not see behind the wall.

Slowly the gates began to open inwards, creaking loudly as though they were rarely used. It was so loud that I winced; it was bad fortune to disturb the spirits during the Spirit Hour, so once it had opened wide enough, we hurried inside.

Once within the walls, the gate was slammed shut behind us by two burly men, making Kamari and I jump in fright. Swiftly the two men slid the crossbar back in place, securing the doors. When they were satisfied, they strode quickly past, grunting at us to follow them.

We walked warily down the long archway leading from the main gates, Dagri's hooves clopping loudly on the cobbled stone floor. Ahead, we could see a section of a village, lit by moon and torchlight. Faces became discernible between the houses as people moved into the light to get a closer look at us. As we drew nearer, their murmured voices reached our ears and their tone was anxious and fearful. It was clear that the sentry had gone ahead and word of an imminent attack had spread rapidly.

We soon found ourselves walking along a path lined on either side by villagers. Whole families stood in nervous silence watching us pass, fear etched in their faces. A woman stepped out in front of me, blocking my path, tears in her eyes.

'Is it true?' she asked chokingly. 'Are we in danger?' I looked at her through my aching, red-rimmed eyes but could offer no words of comfort as I imagined how easily this village would be torn apart.

I stepped around her and continued along the path, feeling, rather than seeing her slump weeping to the ground behind me. My legs were shaking and I stumbled, but my grip on Dagri's reins kept me stable. The village appeared to be built on a hill as the path was now sloping steeply downward, leading us on toward a building that stood out, larger and grander than the other buildings surrounding it. I looked past this imposing structure and from our position I could just about see the rice paddies and animal pens at the far southern end of the village. They reminded me of home.

The two men who had barred the gate were now standing either side of the door to the building.

When they saw us approach, they swung the doors open to admit us, bowing stiffly, their faces as blank and immobile as masks. A young boy appeared and with a swift bow he took Dagri's reins from me and led him away, presumably to the stables where he would be taken care of.

Before we reached the doors I turned to Kamari and whispered quietly.

'We must be polite when we give our warning and perhaps they will give us food for the rest of our journey. And…' Here I struggled a moment for how best to phrase this. 'I know how you feel about the respect due our bloodline but please, do not let them offend you if they do not know of us.'

Kamari looked like he wanted to say something but gave a curt nod instead. We bowed to the two guards before passing through the doors into a large and spacious hall, supported by many circular pillars. The inside was tastefully decorated but really quite humble, nothing like the grand beauty of Lord Hanare's tearooms that Kamari had described to me. Oil lanterns hung from brackets on the pillars and from their light we could see a low rectangular table around which sat five men on faded, well-worn cushions.

They were all nearing middle age but each looked tough and hardened through a life of strict regime and combat. The man at the head of the table had his hair tied in a topknot and his beard was streaked with grey. His kimono was of a deep blood red and although the news of an attack must have reached him his expression was calm and controlled. This was all I could take in at that time as, with a swift look at Kamari, we both bowed to the floor and waited for the man to speak. It was not long before he asked us to sit up in a voice that sounded like he had once had his throat cut. I glanced meaningfully at Kamari who, although trying his best to control it, was looking mutinous at having to bow to this man.

'You are most welcome in our halls,' the man said in his rasping voice. 'Especially as you have been good enough to bring us this warning.'

His gaze passed searchingly over both of us, as though he were somehow able to fathom our innermost workings. I felt uncomfortable as he stared at me, reading me, judging me, but thankfully his silence did not last long.

'I am Haratamo Motsoshige, one of the Overseers of Toramo Village along with these four men - Shey, Darai, Kikucho and Shigenai,' he reeled off the names as he pointed at each of the men in turn. The four men bowed to us as their names were spoken and we returned the gestures. 'What are your names, and what is this threat you have come to warn us of?'

Kamari looked briefly at me and after a pause he gave our answer.

'My name is Kamari Shiro and my friend is Takashi Asano. You may have heard of our ancestors, Deakami Shiro and Timaeo Asano?'

'I have heard the names,' Haratamo replied offhandedly, 'but I know little beyond that.' Kamari managed to keep his voice even as he answered, but I could tell that he had been stung by this casual dismissal of his ancestry.

'We come from a village to the North-West called Aigano, which… was attacked a few days ago by a large army. There is not much left there now,' he said quietly. 'I know also of two other villages they have overrun; Morikai, a small place situated across the northern mountains, and Kirina, a protectorate of Harakima.'

'Kirina has been attacked?' Haratamo whispered.

'Yes… Lord Hanare is dead and I fear most people there met the same fate,' Kamari answered sombrely.

'This is grave news indeed,' Haratamo muttered. 'And we have had no word of it until now. Tell me, did you recognise this army? Have you any idea where they may have come from?'

While Kamari had been speaking I noticed Haratamo casting frequent glances at me. I knew I must look terrible. My lack of sleep had left me disoriented and I blinked over and over to try and steady my vision which was swirling sickeningly.

'I believe they are not from this land,' I piped-up hoarsely. 'Their features were strange, barbaric. I think they have come here from some foreign country, but to what end I could not guess.'

Haratamo was looking at me gravely and in that moment I swayed on the spot and almost fell, but Kamari grasped my shoulders before I could hit the floor.

'Is he alright?' Haratamo asked in concern, getting to his feet as Kamari steadied me.

'He should be fine,' Kamari replied anxiously. 'He just has trouble sleeping and it leaves him feeling unsteady sometimes.'

'Well, if that's all it is, we have a guesthouse he may rest in,' Haratamo said graciously. 'But first I would like you both to have tea with us as a start to our show of gratitude.'

He clapped his hands twice and from out of the darkness four servants seemed to materialise. I was taken aback as I truly had not seen the men standing behind the pillars, waiting upon the five overseers. They set the teacups in front of each of us wordlessly and then disappeared back into the darkness.

'I mean you no disrespect,' said Kamari carefully, 'but the guard at the gate said you have no lords, yet you appear to be treated as such?' Haratamo and his comrades looked at each other before answering. The man known as Shigenai, who had been staring fixedly at the table, raised his head to look at us. He was dressed in a blue silk kimono and had an untidy dark beard and bushy eyebrows that, when combined, all but hid his face. He was well built, not overweight exactly, but he looked as though he had seen better days.

'I imagine the lords you are familiar with decide everything for their people without ever once asking them what they want, what they need, what they think,' he answered slowly. 'We are not like these men. We are merely warriors, artists, businessmen, who have earned the respect of the villagers. They look to us for help and guidance but all decisions are made at meetings, where everyone can have their voices heard.'

Shigenai indicated the pillars behind which the servants stood hidden.

'These men who wait on us are honoured to do so, and one day they may be seated here in our place, guiding the village in our stead.'

'Ah, the tea is here,' Haratamo said suddenly.

Another servant appeared from a side room carrying a steaming pot of tea. He worked his way around the table, bowing to each of us before filling our cups. Once filled we raised the cups before us and bowed our heads to our hosts before draining them. The tea was finer than any I had ever tasted. Rich and herbal, speaking to me of faraway places I had never been. My head felt slightly clearer after taking the tea but I still yearned for a place to rest, away from anyone else.

'Your friend looks a little the worse for wear,' Haratamo said lightly to Kamari. 'He may retire to the guest house now, but I would be grateful if you would return and speak with us a while longer.' Kamari nodded in assent and we stood up together and bowed deeply. They returned our bows and with that Kamari supported me gently out of the hall.

As we exited the building one of the door guards signalled for us to follow him and we did so wearily. The villagers had left the streets and we saw them now through the windows of their houses. Many of them were whispering to each other, watching as we passed. I was reminded of what it had been like to walk through parts of Aigano, but in this case they were not whispering their hatred of me and my family.

It was not long before we came upon the guesthouse which had already been prepared for us. Oil lanterns shone in the windows and the doors had been left open to allow air to circulate. The man leading the way reached the door, bowed swiftly to us and headed back in the direction of the hall. We moved inside and shut the doors against a cold wind that was biting at our heels.

The inside of the house was comfortable, hardly luxurious, but more than adequate for our purposes. Two straw sleeping mats lay on the floor in one room with neatly folded blankets on top of them. In my present state these looked extremely inviting, but as I was about to lie down there came a knock at the door. Kamari shrugged and slid open the door to reveal an elderly woman, her head bowed, a well-piled tray of food clutched in her quivering hands.

'Overseer Haratamo bids you eat before you rest and asks that the one called Kamari return once he has eaten his fill,' she murmured. We thanked her as she set the tray down on a low table and watched as she scurried quickly out of the door.

The food set before us looked delicious. There were rice balls, dumplings and a type of raw fish I had never seen before, let alone tasted. We sat on the floor around the table and ate all we could, this being our first chance to do so for many days.

When Kamari had finished, he sat back and belched loudly.

'I suppose I'll have to go back and talk to Haratamo now,' he said resignedly. I could tell that he was tired by his watery, bloodshot eyes. He was looking more and more like me by the minute. I nodded tiredly as he got slowly to his feet and headed to the door.

'Try and get some sleep,' he said over his shoulder as he slid open the door. 'We've got a long day's journey ahead of us tomorrow.' I watched silently as he closed the door and then listened to the sound of his footsteps receding into silence.

I got to my feet unsteadily and stumbled to my bed in the other room. Removing the swords from my side I threw myself down without taking off my clothes. I gripped the blanket and drew it up under my chin, watching the shadows swirling above me. I felt sure that without a good night's sleep, I would not be able to continue in the morning.

As often happened when I lay down to rest, my mind turned to the question that plagued my life – would my insomnia ever pass? My father had always told me it was merely a phase and would be gone in time – but if anything it had only become worse. There were nights when I would reach a state of desperation as I lay there, unable to drift off, remembering the face of that man...

I turned on my side, trying to get comfortable, and as I did so a wolf howled in the distance, the cry reaching me through the un-shuttered window. An image sprang unbidden to my mind and I saw again the wolf we had seen in the forest. He was howling over the body of his dead mate and as I watched I saw that he was not just a wolf. He was like the spirit I thought I saw earlier... who was a man, yet also strangely not so...

As I looked into the wolf's noble face, I saw something that I recognised, but I could not place what it was because everything had become indistinct as sleep clouded my senses. What I saw in his face, in his eyes, would not become clear to me for a long time to come.

From then on, nothing I saw in my dreamlike state was clear and discernible. As the night drew on, and the moon stared down at me out of a starless sky, I caught glimpses of things that had occurred in Aigano. I saw my family, the attack, my father's body lying on the bridge and the wolves that patrolled the valley. The images whirled and coalesced, as though trying to covey some meaning, but none of it made any sense to me by morning.

I came to with a start, my heart racing and my breathing quick. I did not know what had woken me or even if I had been sleeping at all. Kamari was asleep on the mat at the other side of the room but he awoke at the sound of me sitting up.

'You were saying something again,' he mumbled from beneath his blanket. 'Kept repeating something, don't know what it was.'

Feeling confused, I flopped back on to the mat. Had I been asleep? I did feel marginally better, but sometimes my own imagination appeared like dreams when I was actually still awake.

'What did Haratamo want?' I asked, sitting up again to look out the window.

'He just wanted as much information as I could give him,' Kamari answered wearily. 'He also wanted to hear the story of what happened to us. I was speaking with him until well past the Spirit Hour.'

'What did he say?'

'He wants to talk to us before we leave today. He said to go and see him as soon as we wake, so we'd best be quick, I want to hurry on to Harakima as fast as possible.'

We got up and dressed in the fresh kimonos that had been left for us, then picked up our swords and headed out the door and down the cobbled path towards the building we had first met Haratamo and the Overseers in.

The sky was palest blue and the sun shone down blindingly between patchy white clouds. The Toramo villagers were going about their daily routines as we passed them on the path. There were blacksmiths making weapons, women sewing cloth, the smells of food cooking and all around us were children at play. As we passed, heads turned and a few people bowed. It was clear that they were all grateful for the warning we had delivered. I could tell from the expression on Kamari's face that he was enjoying the attention. This was the kind of respect I knew he had always wanted and expected from the Aigano villagers, but had not received for a long, long time.

I still did not understand why Kamari had ever believed he deserved the respect of the Aigano villagers. I understood the importance of our bloodline and the deeds our ancestors had done, but to my mind, that did not entitle Kamari to the same respect they had been graced with. All the great warriors I had ever read about who commanded respect had earned that privilege, they had not been born with it. Not one of them.

As we neared the building we saw again the same two guards we had seen the previous night. They looked no less stern after a night of rest than they had yesterday. They admitted us silently and we entered to find the five Overseers in the exact same positions we had left them in yesterday. I wondered if they had actually slept at all. Perhaps they had stayed awake, talking over the danger of this threat and debating what was to be done about it.

We bowed to the floor and the pleased expression that had adorned Kamari's face on our way through the village quickly vanished.

'Good morning to you both,' Haratamo greeted us after bidding us to sit up. 'I trust you feel better after your night's rest?' he asked me.

'Yes, I feel well-rested now, thank you.' This was not entirely true, but I did not think it seemly to go into detail of my personal problems.

'It seems we are indebted to you,' Haratamo continued calmly. 'We had heard nothing of this threat before you arrived and without your warning we might have been caught unprepared.' He smiled at us and bowed his head. 'Kamari tells me that he wishes to convey this warning himself to Harakima and as such we have not sent out our own messengers.' I looked at Kamari and indeed he looked determined.

'We have taken this burden upon ourselves,' Kamari answered proudly. 'I will not see the attacks at Kirina or Aigano mirrored elsewhere.'

'That is your wish and we respect you for that,' Haratamo answered and Kamari held his head higher. 'We will provide you with whatever provisions you need for the rest of your journey. We would have given you another horse beside your own, but unfortunately, most of our warriors are now out on patrol.' Haratamo turned and whispered something to his fellows and they nodded in agreement.

'It is your wish that these attacks do not happen elsewhere,' Haratamo said nobly. 'It is our wish that you convey a message to Lord Orran. Tell him that the warriors of Toramo will respond to his call, should he ever need us. We will be here waiting, armed and ready, and we will stop this army in its tracks.' We bowed low after his impassioned words and whispered our gratitude.

Together, Kamari and I left the hall and followed the guards to the main gate. The stable boy stood near the archway, holding on tightly to Dagri's reins. Men and women were strapping loaded saddle bags to the horse and we nodded our thanks to them.

As we started along the archway to the wide-open gates, we turned and saw the villagers had bowed low and were murmuring their appreciation. We stepped through the gateway and heard it close behind us, the heavy wooden bar slotting loudly back into place. We looked to the east and knew that our journey led us there, to the place where Harakima lay.

That was where it would all end.

One way or another.

CHAPTER NINE

Kamari had set a quick pace which I was only just managing to keep up with. He marched on like a man possessed, stopping neither to eat nor even to rest, his gaze fixed unwaveringly on the eastern horizon as I struggled to match his relentless speed.

It was a few hours after midday and still we had not rested. Kamari was now some way ahead and I was left to lead Dagri in his wake. As I hurried tiredly along, my foot caught something in the long grass and I fell, narrowly avoiding being trampled by Dagri's hooves. The sound of my fall seemed to snap Kamari out of whatever thoughts had been driving him so hard. He stopped and turned to see if I was alright.

I had bitten my lip in the fall and blood was streaming down my chin but otherwise I was unhurt. I turned my head where I lay and saw what I had fallen over. I scrabbled backwards in shock as my eyes fell upon the crumpled form of a body lying face down in the grass, blood seeping from somewhere around its mid-section.

Kamari strode up and coldly flipped the body over with his sandaled foot. It was a man – I recognised him instantly as one of the foreign soldiers who had attacked Aigano. Close up his face looked hideous, twisted, almost otherworldly. Were all outsiders this grotesque?

I felt cold with shock at the sight of the body, but as I looked at it, I remembered that only days previously I had pressed my blade against a man's throat and drawn it across, watching unfeelingly as his blood drained into the earth. So why did this sight shock me so?

'I wonder what happened to him?' I whispered, looking up at Kamari.

'Maybe he got into an argument over something,' Kamari said callously. 'Or maybe he fell behind.' Kamari turned and walked away, leaving his words to hang in the air like a dark cloud. The implication of what he had said frightened me. I was slowing him down. I had been slowing him down since the start. He had tolerated it thus far, but his desire to relay his warning was great and his patience was wearing thin. While I knew he was angry, I had also known him long enough to know that he would never hurt me. I was sure that, at the root of it all, he was just worried, and after what he had witnessed, I do not blame him. After that, I walked much quicker and managed to keep up with him, but it was hard-going.

We stopped briefly in the early afternoon, but Kamari said nothing during this time and so we ate in silence. The food given to us by the Toramo villagers was good, hard-wearing stuff; perfect for enduring the bumpy ride in Dagri's saddle bags.

When we were finished, we packed up quickly and continued on our way.

The blue skies above were rapidly disappearing as stone grey cloud banks swept in from the west to obscure the sun. The air was heavy and damp and the earth gave off moist aromas that reminded me of seasons long-since passed. It was going to rain, and by the look of the clouds, it would be torrential.

An hour or so later, it had begun to drizzle and a fine mist descended, lending the landscape an eerie quality. It had become very chilly all of a sudden and so we walked faster to try and stay warm. As the mist surrounded us, all sound became muffled and in this abnormal quiet I felt compelled to speak in whispers.

'We must be getting close now,' I said quietly. 'Have you seen any sign yet?'

'No, not yet,' Kamari answered. As he spoke, thunder rolled loudly overhead, making us both jump. Seconds later, away to the east, a jagged fork of lightning sliced through the sky and in its momentary light, a distinct shape was revealed on the horizon. 'Wait, there! Did you see it?'

'I saw it!' I answered. 'That's it, let's hurry!' We broke into a run and I dragged Dagri along behind us at a quick trot. As we ran, the rain became heavier, pelting us ferociously as we sped towards the impressive shape that could now vaguely be seen against the darkened sky.

A small stream cut across our path, barely noticeable in the gloom and mist, but we vaulted this easily and continued on towards a wooded area that we could not avoid. Two large oak trees stood either side of the muddy path like giant sentinels, guarding the way ahead. Together, we plunged in between the trees, rushing on towards Harakima. Kamari showed no signs of tiring, but my legs were burning and my heart was hammering so fast I feared it would break through my ribcage. The two swords at my side, which had been so light to begin with, now felt like they were dragging me down. As I ran, skeletal branches lashed my face, scoring bloody cuts on my cheeks and forehead, narrowly missing my eyes, but I gritted my teeth and jogged on after him.

Dagri whinnied now and then as branches whipped his body, but there was little I could do to help and, anyway, I could see the trees were beginning to thin-out. Up ahead Kamari had reached the edge of the forest and was now standing stock still.

'I think I can see it,' he said uncertainly as I drew close. 'This fog; it's difficult to make anything out.'

'It must be there somewhere,' I murmured, 'we'll just have to carry on and hope we haven't gone off course.'

We left the trees and continued out into open ground, the heavy rain soaking our already damp clothes. Great pools of water had begun collecting in dips in the landscape and on more than one occasion we stepped blindly into them, the freezing water coming as a shock every time.

It was in one such dip that our small party met with confusion. The rain had begun to slacken-off as another bolt of lightning lit up the landscape and, not far distant, we saw Harakima Castle. It stood against the foot of a low mountain range, its buildings and towers rising majestically against the night sky. Grinning at each other, we fairly hurtled towards the castle, knowing that our journey was almost at an end.

The fog had now become so thick we could not even see our own feet beneath us, so when we unwittingly walked into a huddle of foreign barbarians we were completely unprepared for it. Luckily, however, neither were they. It seemed that they had been engrossed in tactical conversation, but the fierce wind had carried their voices away from us. When I bumped into the back of one of them mid-conversation, he could not collect his wits fast enough to prevent me from, in a flash of anger, ramming him forcibly into his comrades.

We rushed past them as they tumbled to the ground, snarling with surprise and rage. Kamari drew his sword and stood in front of Dagri as I hurriedly rooted through one of the saddle bags, searching desperately for a torch to hail the castle with. I smiled mirthlessly as I laid my fingers upon the handle of a torch and, next to it, two pieces of flint. I wrenched them from the bag and began to strike them together, the drizzling rain making it difficult to kindle a spark. In the time it had taken to do this, the barbarians had managed to struggle to their feet in bewilderment. But their surprise did not last long…

Using my body to keep off the rain I finally managed to light the torch and it sputtered to life. I gripped it in my left hand and began waving it above my head, drawing my sword in the same instant. Together, yelling as loud as we could to alert Harakima, we backed off slowly towards the castle, surrounded by our wavering circle of torchlight, unable to see anything else through the fog.

But while we could not see them, we could certainly hear them.

They were advancing menacingly towards us, their armour rattling, their swords hissing as they slid from their sheaths. Slowly, they appeared from amidst the fog, like creatures out of nightmares. Mist clung to their ragged, muscular figures like the ghostly fingers of spirits and in the torchlight, their faces looked positively demonic. They raised their weapons and began to form an uneven circle around us.

We continued to move backwards as fast as we could manage, as the ring closed in tighter. Dagri was becoming more and more afraid. His eyes were rolling in his head and he was trembling with fear. As they came within weapon range, I looked back at Harakima and waved the torch more frantically than ever, but it seemed that no help would be forthcoming. A face leered suddenly out of the fog and a sword blade whistled by, inches from my face. I turned and swung my sword down violently, watching the firelight playing up and down the blade as it traced an ugly red gash down the man's face. He toppled to the floor, his eyes staring sightlessly into the night sky.

On the other side of Dagri, Kamari seemed to be in trouble. He had cut down one man who had arrogantly ventured too close, but there were more closing in, angry at the death of their fellow. However, I did not have time to dwell on Kamari's situation, for my own was becoming increasingly dire. Three men were bearing-down on me and their faces left me in no doubt of their intentions. I noticed immediately that they were too close together so when the first of them swiped at me with his heavy sword he found his comrade impeded his movements. They were about to shift apart when I made my move, ducking in under the man's second attempt to slice me and rending his chest open vertically, dropping him instantly to the floor. Too late, I noticed I had left myself open to the second of the three men, who wasted no time in cutting my back savagely and kicking me to the ground. The third man kicked me hard in the stomach, knocking the breath out of me before aiming a blow at me with his sword. I rolled away, but his blade tip found my foot and reopened the wound I had got in Aigano, causing me to cry out in pain.

Behind me, I heard Kamari yell in agony and looked over to see if he was still fighting. He was on his feet and, by the look of it, had made a good account of himself, but his left hand was hanging limply at his side and, even from here, I could see blood dripping to the floor. I had released my hold on Dagri's reins some time earlier and until now he had remained frozen to the spot in terror. But at Kamari's shout, he seemed to regain control of his limbs and bolted away into the mist, disappearing quickly from view.

I struggled backwards across the damp ground and found Kamari. We stood back to back and together battled against the barbarians, thrusting and slashing at any face or figure that loomed out of the fog. I cannot count the number of injuries we received while fighting them off hopelessly. That was the first time I ever truly thought I might die. During the attack on Aigano, nothing had seemed real, as though it could not actually be happening. It was so sudden and so unexpected that fear for my own life had never entered my head. But as I felt my body being rent and torn, the realisation that this could be the place I die in hit me like a boulder.

When I could fight no more, I fell away from Kamari and hit the earth limply, believing that I would now pass on to the next world. But at the back of my mind I thought, perhaps I would not pass on? Perhaps I would come back as a spirit like our village elders often said, destined to ever wander this world. I had spoken to Kamari many times about his thoughts on the world beyond and he remained sceptical. I do not think he believed men could come back at all. But I believed, and to me that was all that mattered.

I had dropped the torch and from its guttering light I could see Kamari was still fighting, but it was clear that he was flagging.

It was then that a shadow passed over me. I looked up to see many men running past me to Kamari's side, their weapons raised. One man stood out above the rest. He looked to be around thirty years old. His long, unkempt hair was tied at the back of his head and his jaw was covered with short stubbly hair. His armour reminded me of the warriors I had read about in my books and when he fought, he did so with the strength of many men. I felt a surge of admiration for this man, but that was the last thing I remembered as I felt my head throb excruciatingly, then nothing more.

CHAPTER TEN

A pricking pain in my left shoulder brought me back from the turmoil of my nightmares. The dark, terrifying images I had witnessed in my unconscious state seemed to drip away until I was left with only the vaguest recollection of the emotions they had provoked.

Spikes of pain seemed to prod at random parts of me and I yelped each time it happened, feeling again the barbarians' blades entering my flesh. The feeling of a soft straw mat beneath me made me wonder where I was. I tried to move but I felt a hand at my shoulder grip me tightly.

'Don't move, this will only hurt more.' It was a woman's voice. She sounded quite young, maybe no older than myself. I opened my eyes and looked around. The area was brightly lit. Sunlight flooded the other side of the room, illuminating the latticed screen walls and throwing light on a figure that lay on a mat opposite me. I tried to sit up to get a better look, but again the hands grabbed me and pushed me back down.

'I said lie still, Wolf.' Wolf? My brow furrowed with confusion. Who was this person and why was she calling me that? I craned my neck to look up at her. I saw her hands first. She was stitching a ragged wound in my shoulder in a rough manner that made me feel she was agitated and did not want to be here.

She had quite a plain face, though good-looking in her own way, and her long dark hair was drawn back tightly from her face, almost in the style of a warrior. I opened my mouth to say something, before I had even thought what I was going to ask, but at that moment she finished sewing the wound and told me I could sit up. I did so slowly and achingly, feeling my cuts and bruises shifting painfully. When I felt comfortable, I looked over at the figure across the room and saw that it was Kamari. He looked to be in better shape than myself, although he was still fast asleep.

'I did what I could with your foot,' the woman by my bed murmured. 'But it was a nasty wound. It will heal, but you will be left with a limp, probably for the rest of your life.'

The thought of being stuck with a permanent limp did not seem particularly important right now. I had a lot of questions I needed answering before I could think about that. "Where am I?" and "Who are you?" were of course the most obvious of these questions, but, in the end, I simply said, in a dry, throaty voice, 'How long have I been here?'

'You've been in bed three days now,' she answered distractedly. 'Your friend woke up yesterday and seemed fine, but he went straight back to sleep almost at once.' I looked over at Kamari, who shifted in his sleep and began to snore. I smiled in relief. Kamari was fine; he had always been rather lazy.

'What were you doing out there that night?'

The disembodied female voice seemed to speak from out of nowhere, for I could not see anyone else in the room. I can still remember the first time I heard that voice, clear as day. It brought to mind many things all at once - memories, dreams, emotions; emotions I had felt before, emotions I had never felt and never believed I could. It was one of those things that catches you completely unawares and leaves you speechless, for you could never prepare to hear such a thing. I still hear that voice occasionally, at night mostly, in the dark, when sleep evades me and I lie awake thinking.

I looked around and noticed someone standing behind the woman by my bed. The sunlight did not reach that part of the room, so I could not see clearly who it was. The woman inclined her head to the darkened figure and moved aside so that she could step nearer.

My mind was still full of the sound of that voice, so when I saw who had spoken, I can only imagine the look that must have crossed my face. It was a young woman, she must have been about my age, and the image that her voice had conjured in my mind did not do her justice by half.

Even now, after so much time thinking about it, I find it difficult to describe her beauty. Her hair was shoulder length and darkest brown, the bulk of her fringe tied at the back of her head, leaving the sides to trail down. Her eyes were small but intense, set above a lower lip that was split by a scarlet beauty mark. Her face was palest white; in my village that would have been a sign of ill health but here it only added to her allure. The rest of her features remain stubbornly indescribable. She imbedded within me a level of fascination and attraction I had never known before; they were feelings I had never encountered in my perpetual sleepless state. A realisation came to me that this was the only woman who could ever truly know me, the only woman I could, nay would, ever *let* know me.

'Forgive my rudeness,' she said with a bow, in her voice that only furthered my attraction. 'We have not introduced ourselves. I am Meera Orran, daughter of Lord Orran, and this,' she said with a smile and a joking look at the other woman, 'irritable creature is my faithful attendant, Ellia Kishitani.' Ellia gave her a morose look as she packed away her healing kit. 'What, pray, are your names?'

I was overjoyed. She was the daughter of Lord Orran! Then we had made it to Harakima at last. Thankfully, I found my voice in time to prevent further embarrassment, for I could do little about the look on my face.

'I am Takashi Asano,' I said after clearing my throat. 'My friend over there is Kamari Shiro, a descendant of the warrior Deakami Shiro.' She looked over at Kamari and smiled and I felt a startling pang of jealousy I had never experienced before. I was taken aback and this feeling only strengthened the belief that this was the only woman I could ever love. With a curt nod of her head, Ellia turned and left the room with her healing kit, her expression still inexplicably frustrated. Meera watched her leave with a wry smile.

'Don't mind her,' she said, turning back to me. 'Anyway, I'm sure you want to know where you are. You are in the healing area of Harakima Castle town,' she continued, indicating the space around her. 'It is a building set apart from the main castle, where our injured warriors are cared for. You will be well looked after.' I was not quite sure how to reply to this and so my pause was perhaps longer than was appropriate.

'Why did she call me Wolf?' I asked, unable to think of anything else to say.

'Wolf? Oh, of course, you wouldn't know… You've been in bed for three days and we didn't know your name. We had to refer to you in some way and many of the Kurai said that when they found you, you had been fighting like a wolf.' I was barely able to take this statement in, so tangled was my mind at that point. I was entranced by this woman, all other thoughts and feelings seemed to pale in comparison to her.

When I said nothing, she knelt by my bed to look more easily into my face.

'So, what were you doing out there that night?' she asked warmly and inquisitively. All of a sudden, the reason for our journey hit me like a thunderbolt and I realised that my three days in bed had only wasted time we almost certainly did not have.

I tried to leap out of bed but once again was met with resistance. A strong pair of hands pushed me firmly back to the mat, plainly telling me that I had no chance of going anywhere. I looked up and saw who had stopped me leaving. It was the man I had seen just before I lost consciousness. He was not wearing his armour now, dressed simply in a floor length blue kimono and with his long hair tied in a topknot.

'It will be best if you stay put for now, Wolf,' he said in a low, distant voice that made me feel I could trust him implicitly. 'Can you tell us what you were doing out there?' I did not bother to correct him on my name; I had to get my story out and prepare them for the threat that would inevitably arrive.

'We must all seem terribly rude around here,' Meera cut in quickly, with a slight look at the man. 'This is Shjin Kitano, my father's most trusted warrior. Now please, continue.' I took a breath as I composed my thoughts, then relayed my story.

'We have travelled here from Aigano Village in the north-west to bring Lord Orran a warning,' I began slowly. 'There is a large army come out of the north, from their faces and dress I would say they are foreigners. I could not hazard a guess at how many they number, but they have ploughed a course southward through three villages - Morikai, Kirina and my own. We followed them for a time in a south-easterly direction and came across a village called Toramo, which as yet has been unharmed. This led us to believe they have retreated back north, but given what we have seen so far, we feel sure they will return any time with full strength.' Shjin was silent for some time before answering.

'We already know of this army,' he said grimly as he stared out of the window. 'We fought them for the first time several days ago on the plains north of here. We think they were assessing our strength, but we managed to drive them off alright. We almost missed them too, they were heading south as we patrolled north and we nearly walked right past each other.'

Shjin then went on to describe the ensuing battle and my eyes opened wide in awe and admiration at the courage he and his men had shown that day.

'We thought they were just disorganised ruffians, leaderless and foolish, and at first we did nothing,' he continued, 'but we soon suspected otherwise. We sent out spies to find out what was going on, but... they have not yet returned and now it seems we were right to be worried.' Shjin began to pace up and down as he talked. 'We need to know everything that happened to you; it may shed some light on why they are here and who is leading them.'

'Kamari!' I said happily, looking over at my friend who was now sitting up in bed, bleary eyed and confused, but well.

'What's happening?' he asked groggily.

'We made it to Harakima!' I said excitedly. 'This is Meera Orran, daughter of Lord Orran,' I continued, fighting the strange burst of anger that filled me as Kamari looked at her. 'And this is Shjin Kitano.' Kamari looked at the man, who was still gazing out of the window.

'I was just about to tell them what happened to us, but I can't do it without your help.' Kamari looked suddenly anxious and attempted to leap out of bed and rush to the door. However, Shjin was there to press the struggling Kamari back down to his mat.

'Neither of you are well enough to go anywhere just yet,' he said evenly.

'But we need to warn Lord Orran!' Kamari cried desperately. 'I won't see what happened to those villages happen anywhere else! You must let me speak to him!'

'Anything you want Lord Orran to hear you can tell me first, I am the leader of the Kurai army,' Shjin replied.

'Then you have to tell him of this threat immediately after we have spoken!' Kamari shouted back.

'We already know about the army, what we want to know is what happened to you, in case you have any new information for us,' he answered calmly.

So together, Kamari and I related the entire story of what had happened to us, leaving nothing out, as any small detail could help identify why this army had come to Hirono. When we reached the part where the dying soldier had mentioned "Orran's Blade", Shjin began to pace the room, muttering to himself.

'They could not possibly hope to get hold of it…' He trailed off looking perplexed, but seeing that we were watching him, he bade us to continue.

We finished our story, helping each other through the parts that were difficult to relay to unfamiliar people. The movements of the army seemed to be the thing worrying Shjin the most. There was something in his face that made me think his worries were not solely rooted in the future of Harakima. It looked like some emotion was threatening to burst forth, and he was only just holding it at bay.

'So, they have been taking prisoners in each village they attacked?' he mused aloud.

'Anyone who did not fight was taken captive,' Kamari said bleakly. 'So, in our village, that was most of them.'

'You have said many things that greatly concern me,' Shjin said after a pause.

'Then you must tell Lord Orran at once!' Kamari said heatedly. 'If you will not let us speak with him, then you must tell him yourself, to be ready in case they attack.'

Shjin ceased his pacing and looked down at Kamari as though he could not really see him.

'I will speak with Lord Orran,' he said quietly. 'But I do not expect him to act until after the Spring Festival.' Without another word, Shjin turned and left the room, his loud footsteps on the wooden floor echoing into silence.

'Forgive him if he seems a bit detached,' Meera said lightly. 'He has a lot on his mind at the moment.'

Meera got up from her knees and smoothed down her silk kimono. 'Well, I must be leaving you now. There are a lot of preparations to be made for the Spring Festival; I hope you will both be able to join us. I am honoured to have met you.' As she was turning to leave the room, she glanced back at me. The look was only momentary, but it was piercing, like she was trying to read something deep inside me. I think that our story may have kindled an interest in her, an interest in me...

It was the way she cast the look that was most intriguing. It was fleeting, almost sly, as though she knew she shouldn't look at me like that, but decided to anyway. That look sowed the first seeds in my mind that perhaps she returned at least some of the feelings I felt for her. In an instant, however, she was gone and the room seemed darker without her presence.

'I take it you like her?' Kamari said, grinning.

'Hmm?' I answered offhandedly. 'What do you mean?'

'If your jaw was any lower, she would have stepped on it,' he said, laughing.

'Go back to sleep Kamari,' I retorted with a sideways look at my friend.

'If you don't want to talk about it you don't have to,' he said, smirking. He rolled over on to his stomach and within minutes was fast asleep. His ability to fall asleep so quickly and easily often annoyed me, but now I was happy that I was left alone with time to think.

For the next two days we remained confined to our beds in the healing area. We had been told we needed the time to rest and recuperate but after the first day, the inactivity began to get to me. I wanted nothing more than to leave and wander the castle.

Every so often, Ellia would come and check our wounds were healing properly. Her dismissive manner persisted and when I told her I felt well enough to leave, she firmly told me to remain in bed another day.

Kamari spent most of the time either sleeping or teasing me about Meera, so, to be honest, I enjoyed the time more when he was asleep. I spent most of my time thinking about Meera and wishing I could see her but she did not visit again during our time there. Maybe she did not return my feelings at all? Even so, I spent each sleepless night with all my thoughts focussed on her. I had never felt this way about anyone before. In the past, my sleepless nights were usually spent reading books or brooding on why I could not sleep, so to have something so different to think about was strange. Her image and mannerisms in my mind were so enchanting that I often did not notice when the sun had risen and Kamari had awoken.

By noon of the third day, I had become extremely restless. When were they going to let us leave and speak to Lord Orran? Kamari, however, did not seem to share my grievances, he was still snoring gently, oblivious to everything around him.

It was just as I decided to get up and leave, regardless of what I had been told to do, that Shjin Kitano strode into the room.

'Why are you still in bed at this hour?' he asked with a weak smile. 'You could have got up hours ago, didn't Ellia tell you?'

'I guess it slipped her mind,' I answered wryly.

'Well, you must hurry and dress, Lord Orran will speak with you now.'

Shjin waited patiently outside while I roused Kamari. He did not appear to want to get up until I told him we were finally getting an audience with Lord Orran. At that he was up and dressed faster than I had ever seen him move, chivvying me out of the sliding door without wasting a second.

We stepped into the sandals that had been left for us by the outer door and joined Shjin on the wooden platform that ran around the large building. It was a bright, clear day and the wind that blew between the buildings was extremely refreshing after the cramped and stuffy conditions of the small sick room.

'Welcome to Harakima,' he said warmly with a swift bow of the head. 'We greatly appreciate the information that you brought us.' I got the impression he was still very worried about something but was putting on an air of cheerfulness. He swept his arm around then, indicating the enormous area we found ourselves in. 'The area you are now standing in is part of the second tier of Harakima Castle town. The town is built on the lowest side of the Eastern

Mountains, giving the main castle a good view of the surrounding area. Harakima itself is split into three separate tiers that are divided by thick outer walls. The lowest tier is where the ordinary villagers live, under the protection of Lord Orran and the Kurai. It is there that all our crops and fruit are grown and our animals are kept, so you can see why it is the largest of the three tiers. The middle tier, where we are now, is devoted entirely to the Kurai warriors and their families. If you look north from here, you can see the stables and the training grounds, where our warriors hone their skills.

'The third tier is the smallest of the three, but by far the most magnificent. If you look up and eastwards from here, you'll see Harakima Castle, where Lord Orran oversees the running of, not only the population of Harakima, but the entire Hirono Domain. The castle is also the only place that affords an easterly view over the lower ridge of the mountain, so it provides a good vantage point. Anywhere in the town can easily be defended by the Kurai and our walls are under constant guard, particularly due to the recent threat.'

I looked around interestedly and saw that the tier we stood in was vast and spacious and a veritable hive of activity. In one area there were men practicing with swords and working at grindstones. In another, there were men teaching archery and children being schooled from a book of war tactics. Indeed, no one seemed to be wasting any time, but they did not look dispirited. They all seemed to be working with an attitude other than that of necessity. This atmosphere was peculiar to me, in Aigano none of the villagers had done any work unless they absolutely had to and it directly benefited them or their families. Here, there was nothing of the sort. I was instantly intrigued by these legendary warriors and their way of life. I wanted to discover more about them and their culture, but knew that there were more pressing matters to be dealt with first.

I looked over at Kamari and saw that he was gritting his teeth in frustration. He did not appear to want to know about the layout of the castle. He wanted to tell his story to Lord Orran and felt that we were wasting time, just standing here.

'Come,' said Shjin, apparently noticing Kamari's expression. 'I will show you around briefly on our way up to the castle.'

During our short journey to the castle I saw many things I wanted to investigate at a later time. I particularly wanted to try my hand at archery, as I had never been taught before, but greater than anything, I wanted to learn more about the Kurai and their mysterious customs. Along the way, we saw many boys our own age who were practicing with weapons. They looked at us curiously as we passed; many inclined their heads in greeting, while some simply watched us. We returned the greetings to those who gave them and continued in

Shjin's wake, listening politely as he pointed things out to us.

The wound in my foot hurt me terribly as I walked, forcing me to limp as Ellia had predicted. Pain shot up my leg every time I placed my foot down, but I said nothing of it as I was keen to hear everything Shjin had to tell us.

When we reached the gateway that separated the second tier from the third, we turned and looked out across the sprawling castle town. For the first time I noticed an obvious component of this community that was missing.

'You do not have any shrines,' I asked confusedly. 'How do you worship your Gods and Spirits?' Shjin looked serious when he answered, but it was clear that he was amused by the question.

'The villagers still worship their Gods but we Kurai have no need of them,' he began, looking skywards. 'From birth we are taught to live each day as though we are already dead and through this we are able to serve our lord more efficiently and live selflessly, without greedy thoughts of material gain.' Here he paused as a faraway look came into his eyes. 'To the dead each passing day is precious, each and every moment, and life… seems all the more beautiful.'

I could not help staring at Shjin as he said this. The idea of having no Gods went against everything I had ever learnt in Aigano, but the way they lived made them the most instantly beguiling culture I had ever heard of. I had to find out as much about these people as I possibly could. We turned and headed through the open gate into the third and final tier with Shjin's words ringing in my head.

We passed through the outer wall of the third tier, which was thick and well-fortified; a perfect place to fall back to, should the first two tiers be overrun. A rough stone path led steeply upwards from the gateway, its sides lined by tall and impressive-looking buildings. Shjin pointed these out to us, saying that many of them were guard chambers while some were store houses for food or for weapons. Some of the grander buildings were reserved for visiting lords, who would be greeted there first by servants, before being taken to see Lord Orran. These buildings were also where the lord's servants lived so as to be close at hand, should Orran ever need them.

After a short while the buildings stopped. The path we were following was now sunk into the hillside and bordered by chest-high stone walls that guided it on a twisting route up to the main castle. Shjin told us it had been designed like this so that, in the event the whole town was overrun by enemies, they would be forced along this narrow path, making it easier for the Kurai warriors protecting Lord Orran to fire upon them from the castle. It was a clever defensive strategy, an entirely new way of designing castles that had not previously been put into practice. From here Shjin also pointed out the guard towers that ran along the outer wall, which were used by the Kurai to watch for signs of attack.

At last, the narrow path ended, splitting off into two paths that ran around an ornamental pond upon which lily pads floated serenely. Carp swam lazily in the crystalline depths, passing under the shade of the lily pads. Cherry trees in full blossom grew beside the path, scattering their petals everywhere to form a soft carpet.

Shjin led us along the left path toward the main door and the castle soared above us. It was roughly square in shape and was constructed in numerous different layers, the curved roofs jutting out at each tier giving it a dramatic appearance. The roofs were covered in dark blue tiles which were marvellously offset against the soft sandstone of which it was built, while the window and door frames were of polished cypress wood.

Two guards outside the door bowed their heads to Shjin and after a significant look at Kamari and I, bade us to continue. A servant at the main door bowed to us before sliding it open to admit us. We entered into a small reception area with two small doors leading off to the left and right and one much larger door straight ahead of us. A scrawny male servant was prostrated on the floor by the large door and from this position he spoke to us.

'My Lord Orran will speak with you now,' he intoned in a muffled voice. 'You may enter.' He moved on his knees to the door and slid it open to allow us entry.

Nervously, we followed Shjin into the room, unsure what to expect. The room was expansive; it was clearly the main hall where Orran would meet with other lords and it was far more beautiful than the hall we had met the Overseers of Toramo in. Around the outside of the hall, many paper screens had been placed, their surfaces covered with beautiful depictions of trees, flowers and animals. The skill of the painter was astounding, each and every element was rendered in minute detail. At the far end of the hall sat a man who could only be Lord Orran. He was seated cross-legged on a cushion at the top of a short flight of stairs with a clear view over the entire hall. To my left and right knelt a line of five Kurai warriors facing each other across the room, each wearing a long and short sword at their sides. Two lines of three circular columns stood behind these Kurai, propping up the ceiling, their surfaces covered in breath-taking paintings of waterfalls and birds.

Ahead of us, Shjin indicated the two cushions that had been placed for us to kneel upon, then bowed his head to the floor. As we moved either side of him and bowed down low, Shjin stood and moved to stand beside Lord Orran at the top of the stairs. Too tense and uncertain to sit up, we remained with our foreheads pressed against the cold stone floor.

For some minutes nothing was said as Orran considered us from his elevated position. He seemed quite pleased at our manners when he eventually asked us to sit up, and at last I could get a good look at the famous ruler of Harakima.

He was well over middle age and his black hair, which was tied in a knot on top of his head and held in place with what looked like a tiny dagger, was going grey in many places. He had a neat moustache that ran down into a small plaited beard and his eyes were deep set and shadowed. He was dressed in ceremonial armour which was a mark of his position as lord. He wore crimson breast and shoulder plates, which were intricately designed and crafted, over a black kimono, while a striking short sword rested at his left side. His look and manner gave him the appearance of a man of great strength and wisdom and I knew at once why the Kurai were prepared to lay down their lives for him.

'So, this is Takashi Asano, or Wolf as many know him,' he said, looking at me closely. 'And this must be Kamari Shiro,' he continued, turning his attention to him. Kamari looked up hopefully. I knew what he was thinking. He thought that Lord Orran was going to mention his ancestor; that Orran would treat Kamari with the kind of respect he would have shown Deakami Shiro, so when Orran said nothing more on the subject Kamari's face darkened.

'The information you provided has been most useful in understanding the movements and possible intentions of this army,' Lord Orran said genially. 'We are grateful that you travelled so far to warn us. The hospitality of the people of Harakima is open to you, as long as you wish to stay here. You may leave us now.'

'What!' Kamari almost exploded with rage. 'You called us here simply to thank us? You have not told us what you are going to do about this threat!' To our left and right the Kurai warriors put their hands to their swords and looked to their Lord for instruction. Lord Orran stroked his beard as he regarded Kamari coolly.

'In ordinary circumstances, you would have been cut down for such insolence,' Orran stated mildly, unwilling to be provoked. 'But as you have done us this service, I will overlook it this once.'

'But you must tell us how you plan to deal with these attacks,' Kamari blundered on heedlessly. 'You must call a War Council at once and decide what is to be done!'

'You forget your place, young one,' Orran said, anger rising in his voice. 'Any such meetings will take place after the Spring Festival; I will not have my decisions made for me!'

'But what about Orran's Blade?' Kamari almost yelled back. 'They may have come here to take it!'

'Kamari!' I growled, low and threateningly.

'That is no concern of yours,' Orran snapped back. 'No enemy could ever breach our walls and steal it.'

'I am a direct descendant of the warrior Deakami Shiro!' Kamari retorted loudly. 'You would do well to heed what I say and call a War Council immediately!'

I could not believe what Kamari was doing. If he was not careful, he would get himself killed by any one of the stern looking Kurai warriors kneeling nearby. I knew what emotions drove him to say all this, however. It was clear that the memory of the stubborn village leader at Kirina was filling his mind and I suppose I did not blame him. He just did not want to see another community fall because of one man, who would not listen to the warnings of others. But if I allowed him to continue, he would have us both exiled from Harakima, or worse.

'Enough Kamari!' I shouted, taking even myself by surprise at the volume of my voice.

'My lord, do not blame Kamari for his outburst,' Shjin said by Orran's side, barely disguising his shock at what had just taken place. 'They have been through a lot, both of them. They are simply worried about the safety of those in Harakima.'

'I presumed as much,' Orran said thoughtfully. 'There will be no punishment this time. But know this; if one of my Kurai had spoken to me as you have, I would have had them commit ritual suicide. In this case, I understand that your emotions led your tongue, so I will not require you to do so. It is a few days before the Spring Festival begins, I will have someone show you around until then.'

Orran nodded to one of his servants who hurried out of the room. Then, with a dismissive sweep of his arm, the lord excused us. We bowed to the floor again and backed out of the room, knowing full well it is impolite to show your back to a lord. Shjin followed us swiftly out of the door, a disapproving look on his face.

CHAPTER ELEVEN

'I do not think you have made a very good first impression, Kamari,' Shjin said seriously as we passed out of the castle and into the bright sunlight. 'It was unwise to speak to him like that.'

'But if I hadn't, he would not have told us anything,' Kamari replied, rounding angrily on Shjin. 'We have a right to know what is going to be done about this.'

'I believe it is up to the lord to judge when and how information is given to others,' Shjin answered.

'But we are from noble bloodlines!' Kamari protested. 'Why does he not respect us enough to give us information?'

'He does not recognise your bloodline,' Shjin answered. 'He has heard of your legendary ancestors, yes; but why should that grant you the same respect? Orran judges a man by his own deeds, not by his heritage.' Shjin sighed as though he was thinking deeply. 'Every single one of the Kurai has proven their worth many times over, and yes, I know what you are thinking. Lord Orran is a descendant of a long line of Orrans, but his position was not governed solely by his blood. It was many, many years before he had proved himself worthy to rule the domain. Respect is not given lightly in Harakima, it has to be earned.'

For once Kamari had nothing to say. I believe he had never looked at it that way before. He had always gone through life believing he had a right to this undue respect, so the way of life in Harakima and the rest of Hirono seemed a great surprise to him. I had meant to say this to him many times, but had always worried about the response I would receive.

Without another word, Shjin led us back down the winding, sunken path towards the second tier of the castle town. As we passed through the gateway, I noticed a boy of about our age waiting patiently, apparently for us to arrive.

'Ah, Katsu,' said Shjin jovially upon seeing him. He clapped the boy heartily on the shoulder before turning back to Kamari and I. 'This is Katsu Miyazaki, a young Kurai warrior in training. I'm sure he will show you around and keep you entertained. You've probably got a lot more in common than you might think.'

We both looked at Katsu, who bowed cheerfully to us. He was smaller than myself and quite thin. His hair was fairly short, but what little he had was tied in a knot on top of his head. He had the look of a boy who was often mischievous.

'I must be leaving now,' Shjin said, heading away from us and calling over his shoulder. 'I have much to attend to before the Spring Festival begins.'

Once he had gone, there was a moment of awkward silence between the three of us. It was awkward for two reasons. Firstly, because I had not spoken a word to Kamari since my outburst in the hall and, secondly, because we had now been left in the company of a complete stranger in a place we barely knew.

Katsu, however, did not seem to be the quiet type and he clapped his hands together excitedly.

'You must be Kamari Shiro,' he said cheerily. 'And you must be the one they call Wolf. I've heard all about what happened to you outside the gates, word travels fast around here; one villager tells another and he tells another and so on... you know how it is.' He looked at us expectantly as though waiting for us to say something incredible. 'But I would love to hear a first-hand account of what happened,' he said as an eager prompt.

It did not take long for us to become firm friends with the irrepressible Katsu. He was a difficult person to dislike as he had a knack for keeping happy conversation flowing. He listened with rapt attention as what began as an account of the attack outside Harakima evolved into a retelling of our entire journey thus far. As we talked, we explored the whole of the second tier, which was the perfect opportunity for me to watch the Kurai at work. I was only half listening to the tale Kamari was telling; allowing him to relate the better part of the story.

I think he enjoyed the attention and it looked as though his confidence was returning after hearing Shjin's speech about respect. So, I let him tell the story alone, only putting in the occasional word or two when it was appropriate.

As we continued our stroll, we passed one of the training grounds and I was fascinated to see the discipline of the Kurai warriors. They were practicing with two handed swords, each man perfectly in sync with the timing and fluid movements of every other man's thrusts and swings. They cut striking figures against the long, swaying grass as they span and hacked with their wooden practice swords.

When Kamari had finished our story, it was clear that Katsu was very impressed.

'I have never heard of anyone going through so much, so young,' he said, in quiet amazement. He seemed to be as interested in our lives as I was in theirs. 'Except, of course, for Shjin Kitano.'

'What happened to him?' I asked interestedly.

'Oh, that is a story for another time,' he said. 'I will tell you later tonight.'

'Well, then tell us more about the Kurai,' I said eagerly. 'Shjin gave us some detail about how you live, but I want to know more.' Katsu was quiet for a time while he considered the question.

'It's something that we're taught as children, but grow into as adults,' he began earnestly, watching the men and boys around us training. 'The Kurai life is a strict way of thinking and acting. If you live your life as though you are already dead, you and your soul will always be prepared to die at the hands of your enemies, or at the bidding of your master. It is having this fixed in one's mind at all times that makes a Kurai warrior useful to his master.'

I tried to process his words but the concept was so alien to my upbringing that I found it hard. But I was not given much time to dwell on this as we had arrived at an empty training area. A large rack holding wooden sparring swords stood nearby and Katsu indicated them enthusiastically.

'Ever fought with one of those before?' he asked, smiling.

'No, we've only ever used single handed blades,' Kamari answered before I could open my mouth.

'Let us see how quickly you can pick it up then!' he said roguishly.

We spent many enjoyable hours being schooled in the art of Kurai sword fighting by our hard teacher Katsu. We took it in turns to spar with him and were left with many a lump and bruise afterwards. My foot was still aching painfully, but I tried not to let the pain show, as Katsu might think one of his blows had really hurt me. Kamari looked like he was getting annoyed that he could not land a hit on Katsu, but I was enjoying every minute of it. I wanted to delve more and more into the Kurai customs and with Katsu as our guide, it seemed I would get the chance to.

It was getting on toward evening when Katsu spotted two of his friends walking by after an afternoon of teachings. He hailed them and they strolled over, not least to have a look at Kamari and myself. We were clearly causing quite a stir around the village.

'This is Kamari and this is Wolf,' Katsu introduced us as they approached. 'And these are my best friends Hitoshi and Yohji,' he added, pointing at the two boys who bowed to us. 'They are training to be Kurai warriors like myself.' They were both our age but they towered over us and were extremely well built. It looked as though they kept a strict training regime and it was clear they would become great warriors when they were older. 'Do you want to join in?' he asked them with a sly smile. 'I'm just teaching our new friends here the art of Kurai fighting.'

Long into the evening, we continued sparring at the training grounds. Kamari had volunteered to bow out, as there were uneven numbers, and sat on the side-lines pensively. He seemed rather subdued after telling our story to Katsu. I got the impression he was not becoming as involved in the Kurai culture as I was, perhaps did not want to become involved in their culture. He sat still as stone with a faraway look that suggested he must be thinking of home. Maybe he felt that his loyalties to our home and our upbringing forbade him to mingle with other cultures in this way, particularly the Godless culture of the Kurai. The fact that he would voluntarily sit out of our sparring confirmed this. In Aigano he did little other than train with weapons, for he had never enjoyed reading and believed that manual labour was beneath someone of his bloodline. I was getting worried about him, but I knew Kamari well and was sure that, given time, he would settle down. Everything seemed to have happened so quickly of late that it is no wonder he was a little distant.

I had paired off with Yohji while Katsu was sparring with Hitoshi. It was intimidating to fight Yohji, as he was much bigger than I was, but after a while, I began to predict his movements and learn his style. He still beat me every time in a mere handful of blows, but it was becoming harder for him to land his hits. Just as it was becoming too difficult to see in the failing light, I managed to land a blow on Yohji's shoulder. It was not a hard blow, but of course, with sparring that is not the idea.

He bowed to me and I hastily returned the bow, still nervous to speak to this giant of a boy.

'You fight well, Wolf,' he said approvingly. 'With a little practice you could join us and learn to become a Kurai.' I smiled at this, but before I could answer, a messenger hurried up with a small package and a scroll of parchment clutched in his hand. He looked flustered, as though he had been searching for someone for some time.

'Excuse me,' he began quickly. 'Have any of you seen Shjin Kitano? A carrier bird just delivered these for him and I presumed they must be urgent,' he continued, indicating the scroll and package.

'I saw him heading toward the third tier earlier,' Hitoshi replied. 'He might have gone to check on the stores or he may be in the library.' The messenger bowed his head in thanks and hurtled off toward the third tier.

'What was that about?' I asked.

'It's not uncommon,' Katsu replied dismissively. 'He's often sent messages; it's probably something to do with the army and its movements. He likes to know what's going on at all times to keep Lord Orran informed.'

It was now too dark to spar, so we bade farewell to Hitoshi and Yohji and left the training grounds for Katsu's house, where we would be spending the next few days. We were nearing the door and preparing to go inside, when I heard a noise coming from an area of higher ground to the north. It was lit by torchlight and the sound was repeated over and over - someone was firing a bow and arrow.

'I'm going to see who it is,' I said to Kamari and Katsu, 'I've always wanted to learn to use a bow.'

'Don't be too long,' Katsu replied. 'Supper will be served soon and you'll want to keep your strength up for what I've got planned tomorrow!' I uttered a mock groan and headed off towards the hill. I think Kamari may have suspected who it was firing the bow because he disappeared into the house, whispering excitedly to Katsu and casting many a furtive glance in my direction.

I wandered slowly along the night-darkened path toward the amber glow of the torches. As I drew closer, I stopped short with a muffled gasp and felt my heart skip a beat. It was Meera! Out alone at night, practicing with a bow and arrow? I wondered whether her father knew and approved of his daughter learning the ways of the warrior. As a lord's daughter, I strongly suspected this was not the case.

For a time, I simply stood and watched her, believing she was unaware of my presence. My thoughts had been elsewhere as we roamed the second tier and sparred with Katsu, but now they returned to Meera with startling intensity. The ever-moving flames lit her pale face and for what felt like hours, I was unable to tear my eyes from her.

'You are wondering why I am out so late tonight?' she asked quietly, taking me by surprise. For a moment I dithered, then I swallowed my nerves and took a step closer.

'I was wondering what your father would think of you practicing archery,' I replied, edging closer still.

'He does not mind me learning how to fight,' she answered frostily as she released the taut bowstring. I did not see where the arrow hit as my eyes were fixed on her face, but I heard the soft *thunk* of it striking the target. 'He just will not allow me to join the Kurai, as is my wish,' she continued without looking at me, taking aim and firing a second arrow, as anger pulled at her expression.

'Women can join the ranks of the Kurai?' I asked, bewildered.

'It is very uncommon,' she replied, still not looking at me. 'But my father believes that any who prove themselves worthy to fight should be honoured with that privilege. There are just not many chances for women to prove their worth.'

'Oh,' I said, as understanding dawned. 'Is that why Ellia is...'

'Yes,' Meera cut in swiftly. 'Ellia wishes to join the Kurai too, but she is my attendant and as such, cannot, at my Father's bidding. I know she resents having to wait on me, but I also know that she loves and respects me. She just wants to be given the chance to join the men in battle, as I do.'

'She seemed very irritated when I first saw her in the healing area,' I said, thinking back.

'That was for two reasons,' Meera answered, with a fleeting look at me. 'Firstly, because she thinks a major battle will soon take place between the Kurai and the foreign army and she will not be able to take part. And secondly, because of the way I was...' she flushed momentarily. 'But I mustn't say,' she finished quickly, looking away from me and letting fly with another arrow to cover the silence.

'Shjin said there will be a Spring Festival soon,' I said, upon seeing her discomfort. I was about to continue speaking, but I was surprised to notice that, at the mention of Shjin's name, her expression had changed dramatically. For a moment, some emotion had almost overpowered her, but her will was stronger than it and she had beaten it back. I cleared my throat and continued as though I had not noticed. 'Will you be going to it?' Instantly I regretted saying it. It had sounded much too forward in my head, even before I decided to say it, and the anguished look that crossed her face shocked me. I did not know what this all meant.

'Of course I will be going,' she replied hollowly. 'I am the lord's daughter.' She said this with a bitterness that was impossible to miss. For several minutes we simply stood there, savouring the calm and stillness of the night. Bats fluttered above us, almost imperceptible against the dark sky and the muted flapping of their leathery wings was the only sound we could hear.

'Will you teach me some archery?' I asked casually, moving a little closer to her. She drew away then and bowed her head as though afraid to look at me.

'I'm sorry, but I must be going now,' she said hastily. 'My mother will be wondering where I have got to, excuse me.' She bowed low, then walked quickly away, leaving me alone in the dwindling light of the torches. For over an hour I remained there, teaching myself the ways of the bow and arrow and thinking deeply about what had transpired.

Supper had already been eaten by the time I made it back to Katsu's home. However, his mother, Mila, cooked me some noodles, which I ate hungrily, as I had not eaten since early that morning. She told me that Katsu's father was on the castle walls, performing guard duty and would not return until the morrow. When I entered Katsu's room, I saw that he and Kamari had been talking animatedly about something, but stopped quickly when they noticed me. I was instantly suspicious.

'We were waiting for you to arrive, so I could tell you about Shjin's past,' Katsu said from his seated position on a straw mat. Two other straw mats and blankets had been laid out in the room for Kamari and I to sleep on.

'So come on, who did you see then?' Kamari asked, barely able to hide his mirth.

'It was just one of the Kurai,' I replied hurriedly, not wanting to tell them I had been speaking in private with the lord's daughter. 'Taught me a few things about archery.' A significant look and a smile passed between Katsu and Kamari.

'So, are you going to tell us about Shjin then?' I asked swiftly, hoping to change the subject. I sat down on the mat that was closest to the un-shuttered window and turned my attention to Katsu.

'A lot of this may just be rumour, but it is certainly based on fact,' Katsu began slowly. 'Shjin was not born in Harakima; indeed, they knew nothing of us or our culture in the village he grew up in. It was a village called Kenmui, which was on the far-eastern border of the Hirono Domain. In his village, they kept themselves to themselves and had no dealings with anyone else in the Domain. Their children were kept within the village borders and trained and educated, without ever experiencing the outside world. Shjin was one of these children. It was said that he had no interest in war and spent all his time reading, defying the Elders left and right to try and learn as much as he could about the outside world – a subject it was forbidden to even speak of. In his village they worshipped many Gods and Spirits and their days were spent in hard labour, toiling to please them and feed their families.

'They were not warriors and did not even mount a guard, so they were completely unprepared for what happened that day. No one knew that the battle would be joined there but it was high bad fortune that it was. It began with a man named Shigako Kichibei, a descendant of a lord who had controlled one of the provinces that eventually, under the Orrans' rule, became Hirono. It was he who launched an attack from the eastern border of Hirono, with the intention of sweeping south and west to Harakima. However, our present Lord Orran got word of this attack and sent out one of the largest forces of Kurai warriors ever seen towards the eastern border. Very little was known of Kenmui at that time, so the fact that the two armies engaged there was unplanned by either side.

'The Kurai managed to defeat Kichibei's army, but in the aftermath of the battle, it was clear that few of the Kenmui villagers had survived. It was Orran himself who found Shjin by the butchered remains of his friends and family, covered in blood and unable to speak. From that day, Orran took it upon himself to personally train Shjin and teach him the ways of the Kurai. It was the only way he could think to make up for his part in the terrible tragedy. It was said that Shjin openly accepted our culture, even the fact that we have no Gods. After years of fighting the strict laws of his people, his desire to learn about the outside world was finally satiated through his life in Harakima. Since then, he has served at Orran's right hand and, as far as we know, has never looked back once, nor bore resentment to the Kurai or Lord Orran himself.'

CHAPTER TWELVE

I did not sleep at all that night, but the chance to simply rest was refreshing enough. My mind was full of thoughts of Meera and Shjin. I could not imagine what it must feel like to live and work around the people who were in part responsible for the death of his people. Perhaps that was why he seemed so distant all the time. I remembered seeing a strange look in his eyes when I spoke of the army's movements. Maybe he was remembering the last time an army of this scale had threatened Hirono, and the fatal consequences for Kenmui.

As I lay awake in the darkened room, I reviewed the events of the day and remembered the expression that had flitted across Meera's face at the mention of Shjin's name. There was something happening between the two of them and I felt strangely angry and intrigued by it. More and more, I began to realise how strong my feelings were for Meera, and they grew the longer I thought about her. This was more than mere surface attraction. I wanted to know everything about her, and in turn I wanted her to know everything about me. But the way she left me the last time we spoke made me wonder if she returned any of my feelings at all.

Over the next few days, leading up to the Spring Festival, I saw both Meera and Shjin many times around the second tier, but neither one of them spoke to me. I began to get the impression that Meera was avoiding me, but I caught her one day staring at me from the cover of a building. It happened so quickly, however, that perhaps I imagined it, I had been thinking about her so much. One moment she was there, watching me, and the next she had disappeared from sight.

I tried to push her from my thoughts as Katsu, Kamari and I, and often Hitoshi and Yohji, enjoyed our time together; sparring, talking, learning archery and eating, but it was no use. I tried to tell myself that it was pointless. She was the Lord's daughter and our pairing was impossible. I was not someone of rank or great respect, despite what Kamari may think. But she would not leave my thoughts.

The day of the Spring Festival dawned. A new season was upon us, the season of new beginning and new life, and today was a day to celebrate all life. We used to have similar festivals in Aigano, but they in no way compared to the scale of the celebrations that would soon unfold around me. There was much fevered preparation taking place in each of the three tiers. Huge bonfires were dotted here and there on each tier; some for cooking and others for the villagers and warriors to sit or dance around, to welcome in the new season. No one stood idle. Everyone was doing something, working together to make the Festival a night to remember.

Katsu, Kamari and I helped in whatever way we could to speed along the preparations. I was surprised to discover I was extremely excited, even with all my worries about the foreign army and the situation with Meera. I had never been one for parties, but there was something about the charged atmosphere of Harakima that made me look forward to the Festival more than anything in recent memory.

The night drew on quickly and soon everywhere was enveloped in raven shadows, determined to blot out all light. But they would not succeed, as the bonfires were lit, driving them back into dark corners and the spaces between buildings.

The festivities were opened by Lord Orran himself, who entered the second tier and announced that the Spring Festival would now begin. As was tradition, the villagers and warriors were having separate celebrations - for it was considered improper for the two classes to mingle - but the doors between the first and second tier had been thrown open to allow them to listen to Lord Orran's speech. They crowded around the gateway to hear him welcome in the new season in a voice that easily carried to every person there. To my mind, his speech was short and a little abrupt and, after receiving a prolonged bow from every person there, he spun on his heel and returned to the castle with his Kurai retinue. The villagers watched him leave for a few moments before they got to their feet and headed off to their own party at the centre of the first tier. As I watched Lord Orran leave, it seemed clear to me that there was a lot on his mind.

I did not have long to dwell on this before the raucous sounds of singing, cheering and clapping issued forth from the first tier. The merry sounds brought a smile to my face as our own festivities began in earnest. The food was delicious and plentiful and there were many dishes I had never even heard of before, let alone tasted. There was also a large supply of rice wine that Lord Orran had kindly donated from his private stores. The effects of this drink soon became apparent as tongues were loosened and happy banter hurtled to and fro.

Kamari, Katsu, Hitoshi and Yohji were all deep in conversation. They were discussing their thoughts on possible tactics to employ against the foreign army, should a Kurai attack ever be mounted. The smell of rice wine was heavy on their breath and as they drank, their schemes became more and more outlandish and their words became slurred and unintelligible. Often, they would break out in laughter at the smallest thing and I could not help but join them. But I was only sipping at my wine and soon their conversation was nothing but a dull noise in my ears.

It was then that I noticed Meera. She was sitting across the fire from me, beside her attendant Ellia.

They were conversing in low tones and I do not think she had yet seen me. Many of the Kurai were now seated around the fire, having eaten their fill, and there were calls for stories and poems to be told. One man stood up after much encouragement and cleared his throat. He was old, with grey hair and a face so wrinkled, it resembled tree bark. Many people clapped, while others called for quiet and looked expectantly at him.

'This is a poem called "Wolf Warriors" and I know many of you have heard it before,' he began in a strong voice that mocked his age. There was much more clapping at this; it was clearly an old favourite of the Kurai.

As he began to speak, I looked across the wind-blown fire at Meera and saw that she had stopped whispering to Ellia and was now listening intently. I continued to watch her, as I let the old man's words wash over me.

'White fangs,
Grey fur,
Muscles coiled, ready to spring,
Claw beside blade,
Wolf beside man,
Two races entwined,
Forever allied.

'Enemies come,
And enemies go,

Tooth and steel, set them to heels,
Wolves and Kurai,
Fight side by side,
Protecting Hirono,
From enemy might.

'Death comes to one,
Death comes to all,
Though a warrior's soul,
Can linger on.'

By the last verse, my eyes had left Meera and were fixed upon the speaker, as the poem pierced me deeply. It again brought to mind the wolf I had seen at the edge of the woods on our journey between Aigano and Toramo. Something about him seemed to speak to a part of me. It was a part of myself I had not yet discovered. And for some reason it was a part of myself that worried me; that in some ways frightened me.

It was for this reason I did not notice her approach, so when she spoke from behind me, I jumped and looked across the fire to where she had been sitting. Ellia sat there alone and her expression was disapproving as she stared back at me.

'I see you enjoyed the poem,' Meera said quietly, taking a seat a short distance from me.

'Er, yes,' I mumbled awkwardly as I turned to her, unsure what else to say. She confused me. One minute she's avoiding me and the next she's coming over to speak to me – what did this mean?

'It is a poem the Kurai have been telling for years,' she explained, looking into the fire. 'It tells of the wolves, the warriors of the animal world. They are linked with the Kurai in many ways; their spirits. It is a connection that has bound the two races for generations. There are legends that state a strong Kurai warrior can sometimes return from the dead, reborn in the skin of a wolf; but it is rare indeed.' My thoughts swirled, her words penetrating me deeply, stories the elders had told me about the wolves around our village blending and coalescing in my mind.

Meera turned her head and looked at me out of the corner of her eye in a way that made me shiver. 'You seem troubled.'

I had been so unprepared for her to come and speak to me that I did not know how to react. So many thoughts seemed to be crowding my mind at once – the legend of the wolves, Meera's odd behaviour and the ever-present fear of the foreign army. These thoughts and emotions swirled and churned, threatening to engulf me, but I had to take this chance to speak to her. I took a breath and cleared my throat.

'I'm just worried that the foreign army has been left unchecked,' I said in a rasping voice. 'I think something should have been done about them by now.'

'Do you think my father made the wrong decision to wait until after the Festival?' she asked. I did not know how to answer this because I did not want to offend her. In truth, I agreed with Kamari about calling a War Council sooner, although I would not have disagreed with Orran as he did.

'Would you like to go somewhere else?' I asked quickly to avoid answering. 'I'm too hot by the fire.' She nodded and we stood up and walked away from the bonfire. Even with my back turned, I felt Ellia's eyes upon me.

Together we traversed the second tier and watched the many shows and plays that were being acted out. In one area we found a small stage with a large crowd gathered around it. Actors dressed in brightly coloured, extravagant costumes acted out scenes from stories and legends and performed little comic tales that had the audience in gales of laughter. One actor wore a costume with a false head on top of his own and it was he who drew the most laughs and cheers. Meera and I watched it together and laughed along with everyone else, but my merriment was forced. I was afraid, afraid that someone might see my friendliness with Meera as disrespectful to her father.

I asked her to walk with me and so we left the noise and bustle of happy people and moved to an area that was quieter and more secluded. As we walked, a strong southerly wind carried us further from the festivities, as though guiding us along. When all voices were nothing but a dull roar in the background, I finally felt more comfortable to speak with her.

'I've been meaning to ask why you look so tired all the time,' she said unexpectedly. 'If it is not a rude question?' I considered this for some time before replying.

'I haven't been able to sleep properly since I was small,' I began, but then I hesitated. I did not know whether I should tell her or not. I wanted her to know everything about me, but had no idea if she was just making conversation or if she was really interested in me. On one hand, I wanted to tell her how I felt about her, but on the other, I did not want to be rejected, or worse; offend her and her father.

I still had not decided what to say when a figure strode towards us. It was Lord Orran! My stomach turned over in fear. Was he angry at me for speaking to his daughter? Had I disgraced myself so soon after arriving? Would he have me thrown out, or simply kill me on the spot? All of these thoughts collided in my brain as I stood there, pale as a ghost.

'Meera, your mother has been looking for you,' he said, in a tone I did not like one bit. 'Wolf,' he continued, turning to me, 'the War Council is being held tomorrow and I would like it if you and Kamari could attend. Katsu will guide you there.' He placed a hand on Meera's shoulder and began to guide her away, but before leaving, he gave me a look laced with meaning. It was angry, but protective, the look of a father upon someone he deems unsuitable for his daughter; at least, that was my initial thought.

The morning before the War Council was spent improving our archery under Katsu's guidance. My aim was a little off as I had barely rested the previous night. I had risen many times to take walks in the

night air, but nothing could make me settle. The
fear Orran had instilled on finding me alone with
his daughter was still with me, strong as ever. It was
the look on his face that was most worrying, and
puzzling. It had occurred to me before, but now I
was almost certain of it; there was something big
going on that they did not want me to know about.
But I was determined to understand their behaviour.

The War Council had been set for midday, so,
shortly before, Kamari, Katsu and I set off for the
third tier. Kamari was eager to discover what would
be decided and it was clear he wanted to be involved
in whatever way he could.

'Something must be decided today,' he said,
striding ahead of us. 'They have waited too long
already; the foreigners could be anywhere now.'

'Just... be respectful, Kamari,' I told him quietly.
'We do not want to offend him after he was kind
enough to give us shelter.' I had my own reasons why
I did not want Lord Orran to take any more offence
at us, but of course, I did not say this.

'I will say what needs to be said to get things
done,' Kamari replied grimly.

'Wolf is right,' Katsu piped-up. 'It would be best
if you held your tongue and showed the proper
respect. Men can be cut down for angering lords.'

When we arrived in the hall, it looked exactly
as we had left it, as though the men to my left and
right were statues. I felt great respect for these men,

their unflinching dedication and servitude to their lord was nothing short of astounding. Katsu had not been invited to the War Council and so remained outside, telling us he would wait there for us to leave.

It was clear that the Council had already begun and, as we approached Lord Orran, Shjin shot us a quick glance from his position beside his lord. It was a warning look and it was obvious that it was intended for Kamari. I had not seen Shjin for some time and was shocked to see him looking unwell. He was extremely pale, his face drawn and stricken with anxiety. I had heard he had received more parcels and notes over the past few days and from his countenance, it was clear they had not been full of good news.

'Thank you for joining us at last,' Orran said shortly, as we knelt on cushions placed for us and bowed. 'We were coming to a decision on what should be done about this threat.' He looked around the room and his eyes settled gravely upon one of the men kneeling to his right. The man's expression was angry and reproachful, but he kept his eyes down and did not look at Orran.

'I believe the best course of action we can take is to send out a scouting party immediately, to ascertain the strength and whereabouts of this force. Are we all agreed on that?' There were murmurs of assent from the men around me, even from Kamari, all except the man Orran had looked at. He had raised his eyes and was looking Orran directly in the face.

'But, my lord, we have dallied enough already. Would it not be best to send out an attacking force of Kurai and crush them before they become settled?' I did not like the look in the man's eyes, it was a dangerous look and I turned away quickly so he would not see me staring at him.

'That is enough out of you, Daisuke Inaba!' Orran growled threateningly. 'I will not risk sending my army against unknown numbers. You will accept my decision.'

With quiet fury, Daisuke got to his feet and swiftly left the room. A warrior to his right stood and half drew his sword, looking to Orran for instructions. The Lord waved him down and the man bowed and knelt again.

'My lord, with your permission,' the man who had just knelt said respectfully. 'I do not trust Daisuke. He is always speaking against you and your decisions. I believe there are a great many things he is not telling us.'

'Thank you, Mikao,' Orran replied, looking at the door through which Daisuke had just left. 'I have marked his behaviour and will continue to keep a close watch on him.' Orran flicked his eyes from the door and surveyed the men at his disposal. 'We shall delay no longer; a scouting party must be dispatched and the strength of this army must be discovered. We know they were last headed north, but that does not give us much to go on. The party must be large and must comb every step of the way for any sign of their activities. Gorobei Iesada,' he said, pointing to a man kneeling to his right. 'You will lead the scouting party and may choose whoever you wish to join you.' I looked at the man Orran indicated and was taken aback. Gorobei was a fearsome looking man; ugly and scarred in many places, it was clear he had seen an awful lot of battles. He bowed in acquiescence to his lord and left the room to prepare.

'Lord Orran!' Kamari said unexpectedly and I groaned inwardly.

'Yes, what is it Kamari?' he said slowly. 'Do you disagree with my decision?' he added with a mirthless smile.

'No, it is not that, my lord,' he replied and I looked at him, perplexed. What was he up to now? 'I was merely wondering if I might accompany the scouting party? I would like to help in any way I can.' Lord Orran raised his eyebrows and looked amused at the request.

'You have spirit, Kamari,' he said approvingly. 'But I cannot allow you to go, you are too young. Not even the Kurai boys of your age would be permitted to go.' Orran smiled at the crestfallen look on Kamari's face. 'But if you would like, you may perform guard duty on the wall tops. That is something all young warriors take on during their training.'

To my relief, Kamari did not look angry or overly upset at the decision; he simply nodded his head and bowed.

'Now, let us waste no further time on words,' Orran said looking around the room. 'You all know what you must do, so you may leave.' Each man bowed his head and then silently left the hall, facing their lord as they did so, their eyes respectfully downcast. Kamari and I followed at the rear. Shjin, however, remained behind, speaking to Orran in a low voice. As I backed out of the room, I glanced up and saw that Orran was listening and nodding to everything Shjin was saying, but his eyes were fixed on me. The memory of his face on seeing me alone with his daughter reared suddenly in my mind. Hurriedly, I left the hall and caught up with Kamari and Katsu.

Kamari wanted to begin watch on the wall tops immediately and so Katsu asked his mother to bring us up some food for the midday meal. We had been assigned to watch from the northern wall top of the first tier. We were greatly honoured to be given such a post, as it would mean we could keep a look-out for the return of the scouting party. We would not be entirely on our own up there, of course; there were other men stationed there who would be able to help us if we needed it.

This was the first time I had walked through the lowest tier of the castle town and so I finally had a chance to look around. The houses here were small and not as well-built as the warriors' houses, and appeared to have been positioned haphazardly, with no thought to order. The patchy grass beneath my feet was strewn with hay and animal droppings and I could see many men and women leading horses and oxen. After spending most of my time in the second tier, it was like stepping into another world; so different to the order and discipline of the warriors' tier. But the people did not seem unhappy. They were working hard in the rice paddies and singing while they did so. Women collected water from wells that were filled from mountain springs beneath the village and sounds of talk and laughter buzzed on the air.

As we passed through the village to the wall steps, many of the villagers smiled and bowed to us, some even called out greetings which we returned readily. I think Katsu felt a little uncomfortable mingling with the villagers. He was a warrior's son, a Kurai in training, and it was a general rule that the villagers and warriors did not mix. We reached the steps and ascended to the wall top. A Kurai guard issued us with a small horn and a longbow and quiver of arrows each, before leading us to the area of wall we would be patrolling.

The hours stretched out before us, seemingly endlessly, as we remained on guard for the rest of the day. We had watched as the scouting party left by the main gates and spread out, heading north on horseback, but since then, nothing had happened. I had thought that Kamari would have tired of this quickly. He surprised me, however, by appearing happier than I had yet seen him at Harakima. I think the fact that he was doing something constructive was the reason for this. He roved the walls ceaselessly, speaking with the other Kurai guards and straining his eyes to be the first one to see something unusual in the darkening landscape.

While Kamari kept himself busy, my thoughts returned to the legend Meera had spoken about during the Festival. Katsu was standing nearby so I hailed him and he walked over.

'The other night at the Festival, someone told me about the legends surrounding the Kurai and the wolves...' I began, but before I could say any more, Katsu had already jumped in. Clearly this was a topic he was greatly interested in.

'I loved those stories when I was a child,' he said, eyes alight with wonder. 'My grandfather used to tell me them every night. Only the strongest Kurai earn the right to return in the skin of a wolf. It is said they return so that they may go on protecting the Orran line and the Hirono Domain, even after death. Grandfather often spoke of some kind of... conduit... a wolf whose job it was to watch over and usher these Kurai spirits to their new homes.'

'Have you ever seen one?' I asked in a hushed voice. Katsu shook his head.

'No one has seen one for years,' he replied. 'My grandfather thinks they may have all died out, but I don't believe that.'

I turned away from Katsu and looked out over the wall. I could only imagine the strength of a warrior's spirit that could endure, even after death, to continue fighting for what is right. I hoped with all my heart it was true.

Night fell eventually, as we conversed in low tones while gazing out expectantly into the coal-black shadow. But the time passed uneventfully; nothing was seen nor heard at all during those long hours. It was during the Spirit Hour that it had been most silent. Kamari and I spoke very little during this time, as we knew it was best not to disturb the night.

By morning, I noted with a wry smile that Kamari and Katsu were fighting a losing battle against sleep. Indeed, Kamari looked pale, as he rarely spent whole nights awake. Katsu seemed to be a little better, as he had done guard duty on previous occasions, but he still looked as though he was desperate to lie down. I had not slept at all during my time at Harakima, so the hours spent awake were nothing out of the ordinary to me.

Three guards arrived early in the morning to relieve us and Kamari and Katsu gladly accepted, but I knew I would not sleep anyway and so decided to stay on guard.

I spent the rest of the day alone, brooding on everything that had happened during my time at Harakima. Katsu's mother brought me a bowl of rice and a small bottle of rice wine to keep out the chill, but other than that, I spoke to no one. I wondered what could be happening far to the north. Had the army been found and their strength ascertained? Was a battle being waged even now? Or had no trace of them been found and would they return empty handed? Secretly, I wished I had been allowed to join them, as Kamari had wanted. After seeing what this army was capable of first hand, I knew that further attacks would be devastating and wanted to aid the Kurai as much as I could.

The day passed quickly and, buried deep in my thoughts, I did not notice that it was already evening. A movement below and the sound of ragged breathing made me lean over the wall top and peer intently into the shadow. Somebody was heading toward the castle at a run. Judging by the erratic nature of his chosen path the figure was alone and frightened. I hailed the guard closest to me and he hastened over to stand at my side. Other guards, upon hearing my shout, hurried over also.

'It is Gorobei!' one guard with sharp eyes said worriedly, leaning right out over the wall for a closer look.

'Are you sure?' another asked, straining to make out the figure.

'I'm sure,' he replied, with a frown, 'but he is alone. What has happened?'

'Open the gates!' another man yelled down to the door guard. 'Gorobei has returned!'

Gorobei Iesada was a terrible sight to behold. His hair was matted with blood from an unseen wound and a long gash ran down his left arm. His face was a picture of horror and fear, but his eyes held an emotion that did not match this expression. There was something horribly wrong about the way he was looking at everyone.

Gorobei was half carried, half dragged up to the castle and taken into the main hall, where Lord Orran was awaiting his report. One of the warrior's wives, who was skilled at healing, tended to his wounds as he knelt painfully before his lord.

I had followed the party to the castle, stopping only to rouse Kamari and Katsu, who had still been asleep. Together, we hurried up to the castle and the urgency of the situation was such that they did not notice us enter the hall to listen to Gorobei's account.

'Gorobei, you must tell us what you discovered,' Orran said, quietly but insistently. 'What happened to the rest of the scouting party?' Gorobei hung his head and when he spoke his voice sounded shamed and distressed.

'At first, it appeared we would find no trace of them,' he began slowly and haltingly. 'But just as we were about to turn back, we found a large body of tracks coming out of the west and heading north, so we followed them. I wish now that we had not...' He seemed as though he could say no more, but just as Orran was about to press him further, he began to speak again. 'My lord, they have built a fortress close to the foot of the Northern Mountains - it seems they are using men and women from the villages they have attacked as slaves.' At these words my hopes were rekindled. I had thought very little about my family since I had left Aigano, as it was too painful to do so, but now I knew there was a chance they could still be alive. Even now they could be straining under the lash of those barbaric foreigners.

'However, the fortress is not fully complete,' Gorobei continued. 'We moved in for a closer look and I was able to discern their numbers, when… when we were attacked. They took us completely by surprise; we did not stand a chance against them. I watched as my men were cut down around me and… my lord… I ran. I ran until I could no longer hear the sounds of their deaths. I knew that I must tell you what I had discovered, but that does not excuse my cowardice. I should have stayed and died with my men.' At this, he prostrated himself on the floor in front of Lord Orran. 'I am eaten up by shame and feel I have lost my honour this day. My lord, I offer you my life as payment for my cowardice.' Orran looked down on him sorrowfully as he answered.

'Gorobei, you acted correctly this night. At any other time, it would have been most honourable to die in battle, but not this day. The information you have discovered is worth far more to me and the inhabitants of Harakima than an honourable death. I do not accept your life as payment for your actions. But now you must tell us of their numbers.

How strong a force are they?' Gorobei raised himself from the ground and it was clear that it pained him to do so.

'My lord, they have a fortress to hide behind and they are strong and wily indeed, but their numbers are no match for the full force of the Kurai. If you were to march on them today they would fall easily before...'

Gorobei was cut short by a sudden sound that drifted through the doors on the chill evening air, causing everyone in the hall to freeze. The sound was repeated - a horn call from the north, long and low. Every man there tensed as the frightening reality hit them.

'I was afraid of this,' Gorobei murmured in a low voice. 'My lord, before we were attacked, I also saw the leader of this foreign army.' Orran said nothing and simply stared at Gorobei. 'It was Zian Miyoshi, my lord. He has returned to Hirono!'

Shock and confusion flitted across Orran's face and it was obvious his mind was racing. Again, the horn call echoed out threateningly, louder and longer than before.

'They are attacking, my lord,' Gorobei said earnestly. 'Zian has sent his army against us!'

CHAPTER THIRTEEN

All was confusion as the Kurai defenders rushed to the wall tops armed with longbows and quivers of arrows. Kamari, Katsu and I surged along with the other warriors and were soon joined by Hitoshi and Yohji, who had come out of their houses to discover the source of the commotion. With grim expressions, we ran silently side by side - rage and anxiety coursing through my veins, as the thought of my family being used as slaves filled my mind.

When we reached the wall steps, I was handed a bow and grasped it eagerly. I had thought we would be sent away - shut out due to our age - but I think, in the heat of the moment, we were united by our common intent and age no longer seemed to matter. When we finally made it to the battlements and looked out over the wall, the sight that met us was both awe inspiring and terrifying. In the dark of evening and from this great height, it looked as though a wave of fire was racing towards the castle, threatening to break itself upon the walls. As the wave drew closer, this vision was dispelled and I could see that there were hundreds of men bearing lighted torches, heading directly for us. The light from the torches was dazzling and I knew that if they continued to hold them, it would be difficult to fire on them with any degree of accuracy.

The battlements were now bristling with Kurai warriors. They filled every available space of the walls on each tier of the castle, waiting expectantly for the attack to begin.

The advancing army came to an abrupt standstill just outside our weapon range and held their torches aloft. For a few moments a tense silence fell - then all at once I heard that nightmarish sound again. That sound had echoed in my mind ever since the attack on Aigano, but I had hoped never to actually hear it again.

Clack! Clack! Clack!

With their free hands the foreign barbarians beat their weapons against their helmeted heads and roared their defiance up at us. From their ranks, a man stood forward and I recognised him instantly. It was the tall man who had stood before my father and I on the bridge in Aigano. The man who had ordered his soldiers to murder Yaram, Takeda and my father. The man who had left for me dead.

It is said that warriors mark their targets in battle like a hawk; that when they enter into the fray, they give no heed to any other than the man they first marked. I knew now the full truth of this as I fixed his image in my mind and pledged that I, and no other, would be the one to bring him down.

I watched as he raised a horn to his lips and blew three long blasts - the signal to attack. At once, the army flooded forwards, passing around the man like water around a rock, but I barely registered them. As the Kurai strung arrows to their bowstrings and began loosing them at the army below, my eyes remained locked on that man – he was the only thing in sharp focus.

I pulled an arrow from my quiver and took aim at the man as he continued urging his men forward, lashing out at those moving too slowly. My focus narrowed to a point – nothing else existed in the world but my arrow and my target. I took a breath… and let my arrow fly. But in my anger I had misjudged. If I had been thinking clearly, I would have realised that he was still way out of range, so instead of hitting him, my arrow struck another soldier, piercing him through the neck.

The world returned to focus like a thunderbolt and I realised they had reached the castle walls. Their ranks parted to reveal many tall wooden ladders, which they began to raise, protected by men with shields. I took my eyes off the man for a moment and watched as Kamari and Katsu whipped arrow after arrow into the masses of soldiers below. To my other side Hitoshi and Yohji were doing the same, aiming their fire at the men raising the ladders.

Only a moment had passed, but when I looked back I saw that the man had gone. Desperately, I searched amongst the seething horde below and easily spotted him, so vivid was his image in my mind. He was heading to a group nearby who were raising a ladder and had unwittingly come within my range. I trained my bow on him and fired, watching the path of the arrow breathlessly. My aim was off and the shot was not fatal, taking him squarely through the thigh. But the wound did not seem to affect him. With one tug he ripped the arrow out and sneered, hurling it away from him as he began to climb. I quickly strung another arrow and fired again, but this one only grazed his shoulder and continued on its path, striking another man who did not see it coming.

Angry with myself, I drew one of my few remaining arrows and took more careful aim. He was over halfway up the ladder and the men on the wall top could not seem to tip it over. Arrow after arrow thudded into his flesh but he continued to climb relentlessly, like one possessed by demons. I could see his face clearly now, contorted by rage and pain and bloodlust. My hands were shaking and I tried to steady my breathing as I prepared to take the shot. I narrowed my eyes to slits and the world faded away once more until all I could see was him. I loosed the arrow and it whipped harshly from by bowstring. He was just straddling the top of the ladder when my arrow found him. With a sickening sound that was lost in the clamour of battle, the barbed tip penetrated his skull, passing through his brain and emerging through his left ear.

Instantly limp, his body toppled from the ladder, dislodging the men climbing below him and crushing many more as it hit the ground. As though a veil had been lifted from my eyes, I was able to see clearly again and the men below came back into focus. Instinctively, I reached for another quiver of arrows and began firing non-stop into the attackers.

As the battle raged, some of the more courageous villagers rushed between the Kurai soldiers, handing out quivers of arrows and tending to the wounded. An arrow had passed right through Katsu's wrist but he shrugged off all aid and continued to fight, his jaw clenched in agony.

In the heat of battle, I had not noticed that, to my right, Hitoshi and Yohji were in trouble. A ladder had been positioned directly below them and, try as they might, they could not hold-off the men who swarmed up it, cursing and screeching in their heathen tongue. It was as I turned to check on them that they were finally overwhelmed and cut down. They fell with their bodies facing the enemy, fighting to the last. Katsu, who had turned at their cries, screamed in anguish and collapsed to his knees, shuddering violently, staring horror-stricken at their bodies.

'Kamari!' I yelled, causing him to spin around. Kamari took in the scene in an instant and sprinted over.

With Kamari at my side, I drew my sword and threw myself at the men climbing off the ladder. Our blades met theirs and we dispatched them quickly, kicking their corpses over the wall and into the crowd below. Together, we shoved the ladder away from the wall and watched it spin awkwardly down into the panic-stricken foreigners.

The sounds of battle were suddenly cut short when a horn call sounded from the east and an answering call from outside the gates swiftly followed. At once the men began to retreat, leaping from their ladders and fleeing northwards, away from Harakima. We shot arrows at their retreating figures until we could no longer see them in the darkness.

The aftermath of battle was almost worse than the battle itself. Many men had fallen that night, friends and strangers alike. It was a time for grieving, and for anger. While I felt great sorrow for the loss of Hitoshi and Yohji, it was even more heart-wrenching to look upon Katsu now. Seeing his two friends die had left him in an advanced state of shock the healers had never before seen. He lay on his mat as rigid as a board, his eyes glassy and staring, as grief gripped him in powerful hands. He seemed unable to do or say anything and simply lay there; his face pale and drained as though it were he who had died. A woman had bandaged the awful wound in his wrist, but he did not seem to feel the pain at all.

Orran himself had come down to the lower tier to witness the fallout first-hand. He walked amongst the myriad bodies, his fists clenched tight as though they ached to pick up a sword. He stopped here and there to kneel by an injured man and whisper words of comfort and encouragement.

Kamari and I sat with Katsu, both of us weak and trembling now that the din of battle had faded. We could find nothing to say to each other and simply sat in silence, trying to come to terms with what had happened.

'My lord! My lord!' A soldier from the castle came tearing down the path to Lord Orran, who turned anxiously at the sound of his voice. Orran had been speaking to a man close by and so we heard every word that was said.

'Lord Orran, I bring terrible news,' he said, in a voice so frantic I felt terror claw its way up my spine. 'I cannot think how it has happened… We must hold a council now, away from all these people.' It was a measure of his great strength that Lord Orran showed no visible sign of anxiety. He got quickly to his feet and for a moment looked as though he wanted to speak, but then he changed his mind and simply nodded his head, indicating that the soldier should lead the way.

I felt torn. I did not want to leave Katsu's side but I had to find out what was going on. We made sure he was comfortable before we hurried off in the wake of Lord Orran and the soldier on their way to the castle. *What could have happened?* I kept wondering to myself as we jogged to catch up with them. *What could be more terrible than the death of all these men?*

When we got to the hall we found that everyone had already assembled. I noticed with great sadness that there were many empty spaces among the Kurai soldiers lining either side of the hall. But only two of the missing could I identify. Firstly, I noticed that Daisuke Inaba was not in his rightful place to my left. With concern I also realised that Shjin Kitano was not standing at his lord's side.

Orran did not seem to mind that we had invited ourselves to this emergency meeting. In fact, when he first spoke, he spoke directly to us.

'It seems we should have taken your warning more seriously,' he said hollowly, staring fixedly at the ground before us. 'It grieves me terribly to say this, but… Orran's Blade has been stolen.' There was a sharp intake of breath from the kneeling Kurai soldiers. 'How this could have happened, I do not know, but it seems obvious that this was Zian's goal from the start. We must all now face the stark truth that it would not have been stolen if it were not going to be used.' Whispers broke out around the hall like wind through a cornfield. It was clear that many there knew the seriousness of these words, but there were also many blank faces, mainly on the younger Kurai. Orran held up his hands for silence and continued.

'I suppose the importance of this needs explaining, not just for Wolf and Kamari, but for some of our younger Kurai who may never have been given the full truth of the matter.' He looked around forlornly and it seemed that an air of hopelessness had settled in his heart. The cool, collected man I had seen only minutes prior was gone and a different, deflated man sat before me. He took a deep breath before he next spoke. 'The Blade harks back many, many years to the days when my ancestors first took control of the provinces and united them into the domain you know as Hirono. At that time, far to the east, the land was riddled with lakes and great ravines. No one approached these waters, indeed no one lived for miles around for fear of these lakes and the stories that surrounded them. It was said that mighty Water Dragons lived deep in their murky depths, in caves far below the surface, away from prying eyes.'

Dragons! For a moment I thought I must have misheard. *Dragons?* I had heard legends and stories about them but never, in my wildest imaginings, had I actually thought they were true.

'The official records from the time of the Dragons are now all but lost, and those that remain are vague and unsure. But what is known is that man's fear is a powerful thing. One by one, the dragons were starved-out or killed-off until only one remained, the greatest of the Water Dragons - Aralano. Enraged at the deaths of his brethren and driven to the brink of madness, Aralano embarked on a massacre, the scale of which has been unrivalled throughout history. Many hundreds fell before his steel claws and icy breath. There are even accounts of the beast taking control of water wherever he found it. Indeed, reports from the time tell us that many villages were washed clean away, so terrible was his lust for vengeance. I am ashamed to say that my ancestors thought less about killing the beast and more about his capture. You see, these events occurred shortly after the unification of Hirono and the ever-present threat of retaliation from the exiled lords was constantly on their minds. They felt sure that if they could somehow harness Aralano's power, no one would ever dare challenge their rule.

'It was for this reason that the last of the sorcerers, a dying breed in a modernising world, were summoned to Hirono to trap the beast.' Orran sighed deeply as the memories washed over him. 'After much bloodshed, Aralano was finally captured and imprisoned within a gemstone, set into the hilt of a dagger that had once belonged to the first Lord Orran. The dagger was chosen as a powerful prison, for it had taken many lives and shreds of men's souls still clung to it. It was these souls that bound Aralano to the blade and allowed the one who wielded it to control him. But so great and terrible is his wrath that for many long years the blade has remained, ever under guard, present now only as a deterrent against invaders.' At this point Orran paused and looked around to see that every man present had his eyes trained intently on his face. I was fascinated and terrified at the same time, knowing that the man who held my family captive could now command the power of this dragon. The fury of Aralano could be visited upon Harakima at any time, and what could we do to stop it?

'Zian Miyoshi,' Orran fairly spat the name. 'The man who is responsible for all these attacks over the last few weeks,' he continued, his fists clenched. 'He was once a Kurai warrior, about ten years ago now, but he did not truly believe in our code or follow it as was his duty. We never have, and hopefully never will, require contact with men from the outside world, but Zian believed that the only way to better ourselves was to advance our knowledge and technology by opening our borders to foreigners. Our code decrees that you shall look for nothing more in our way than what is already there, but he was not content with this.

'His interest in Orran's Blade was worrying. He would spend days at a time with Daisuke Inaba, poring over scrolls in the library, but I never discovered how far he got with his investigations. His behaviour became increasingly erratic until I could stand it no longer and put him under close watch. It was one winter that he was discovered at the port of Kagashi, on the far-northern border, conversing with foreigners. He knew our code forbade such dealings. As punishment, he was exiled from Harakima and for years he has not been seen in Hirono. It seems obvious now that he has spent these past years overseas. When Gorobei told me who was leading this foreign army, my thoughts flew at once to the Blade, but I did not for one second think he could devise a way to breach our walls and steal it. But then, he did not breach our walls at all... did he?' Orran looked over at the soldier who had brought him the message about the Blade. 'Koba, tell me what happened. While you were guarding the Blade Room this evening, did anyone at all approach it?'

'Yes, my lord,' he answered humbly, his face full of shame. 'Myself and Milau were on guard when he approached us. We thought nothing of it when he bade us take a break and eat something. He often does so and thus our minds were not troubled.'

'Who?' Orran asked harshly. 'Who approached you?'

'Shjin, my lord,' Koba replied nervously. 'It was Shjin Kitano.' My blood ran cold.

'Shjin!' Orran said aghast. 'No... Shjin would never steal the Blade! He has served me faithfully for years! Did no other approach the room while you were there?'

'Yes, lord, there was one other.'

'Then tell us! Who?' Orran almost shouted.

'Daisuke Inaba, my lord,' he answered swiftly. 'He passed us shortly after Shjin relieved us, but we did not see him leave. When Shjin did not come back, we returned to the Blade Room and discovered it had been taken.'

'But then it makes sense!' said Orran. 'Daisuke was friends with Zian and they shared an interest in the Blade. They must have been working together to steal it - they seek control of my domain! Where are Shjin and Daisuke now?'

'Both are missing,' another man piped-up. 'They have not been seen since the Blade Room.'

'Shjin's disappearance is not unusual,' Orran murmured. 'He often leaves to gather information, but the disappearance of Daisuke? How long ago was that?' he asked quickly.

'It was during the attack, shortly before they retreated,' Koba answered.

'Just before they retreated, there was a horn call from the east,' Kamari said unexpectedly, and everyone looked at him. 'Maybe that was the signal the Blade had been taken and the attack could be called off?'

'Then we have precious little time left,' Orran said, getting to his feet. 'Gorobei - you said their numbers were no match for the full force of the Kurai, is that correct?'

'It is, my lord,' he answered respectfully. 'Against the full complement of the Kurai, they would surely fall.'

'That may be true, but I do not believe in taking chances with the lives of my men,' he answered and Gorobei's face darkened. 'Send out our fastest messenger to Toramo immediately. They offered their support and now I will gratefully accept it. We leave tomorrow as soon as they arrive.'

CHAPTER FOURTEEN

It was still dark and an icy wind whipped my face refreshingly, helping to banish the heat left from battle. I walked alone as Kamari had gone back to check on Katsu and get some rest, ready for the morning. After the conversation we had just had with Lord Orran, I knew sleep was impossible and so had decided to stroll to the walls, feeling my stomach knot with apprehension. It had taken much persuasion, but Orran had eventually given-in and granted his permission for us to join the Kurai and confront Zian. I was more than a little surprised at this. I felt sure he would do all in his power to stop us - citing our youth and inexperience - but in the end he relented when we told him that, even without his permission, we would be going, one way or another. He realised that whatever he did, we would find a way to go and so gave us his permission, although, strangely, it looked as though it grieved him to do so.

I sat now on the wall top, my legs hanging over the edge, staring north to where our journey would lead us tomorrow. I had already watched the messenger leave on horseback, galloping away in the direction of Toramo, and was now left with nothing to do but wait.

So much had happened that I did not know what to think about, but paramount amongst my thoughts was, what had happened to Shjin? I did not believe for one moment that he was responsible for stealing the Blade. On first sight, I had felt that I could trust him completely and everything I had seen of him since had only strengthened this feeling. But then, I had often seen a strange look in his eyes that spoke of worries unvoiced. Since arriving at Harakima, I had realised there was a lot to be discerned from peoples' eyes. Many times now I had seen things in people that led me to question their motives, whatever their words or deeds might say to the contrary. For instance, the look I had seen in Daisuke's eyes when Orran had refused to attack Zian at once. It was anger I think, but then what was its source? Was it Daisuke who had stolen the Blade for his friend Zian? Had some plan been ruined when Orran would not attack at once? By this point, my head was reeling from all the possibilities and so I looked up into the night.

A quarter moon hung low in the inky sky surrounded by millions of stars, as though it had long ago exploded and showered its glittering fragments across the heavens. I looked at the stars and tried to pick out the shapes I had read about, like that of The Great Wolf, but my thoughts kept turning to Meera. I had not seen her since the night of the Spring Festival and now any time spent away from her felt empty and hollow.

As though I had been voicing these thoughts aloud, I heard someone approaching quietly along the wall top.

'It is a beautiful night,' the voice said, close by. 'It is strange that so much evil could happen under a sky so wonderful.' It was Meera! Of all the people to have sought me out, I never would have expected it to be her. Yet again, she had instantly confused me. She had clearly been avoiding me for days, so why had she suddenly come searching for me in the dead of night? I did not understand her at all.

'Indeed,' I answered, glancing at her. 'Much has happened this night, many have fallen; and it seems this will not be the end of it.'

At this Meera said nothing. It was clear she had been grieving; her eyes looked red and swollen, but a fierce anger burned there also.

It surprised me when she moved towards me and sat by my side on the wall, dangling her legs over the edge. For a time we were both silent, enjoying each other's company without the need to speak.

'You never did answer me,' she said slowly, 'about why you look so tired all the time?'

Right then I knew what had driven her to seek me out. This was... fate, this was destiny – call it what you will, but this was meant to happen! Now was the moment to finally tell her how I felt about her. But I did not know how to go about it without offending her or embarrassing myself.

'Meera, I wanted to…' I began, but I got no further as Meera placed her hand in mine.

'I know how you feel about me,' she cut across me quietly, looking down between her feet at the dizzying drop below.

'You know?' I asked, bewildered. 'But how…'

'You could not have made your feelings more obvious,' she said with a wry smile, 'it was not only me that noticed.' I felt sure that smile would be the end of me. In that moment I also had the sinking feeling that she did not return my affection.

'Is that why you've been avoiding me?' I asked with a heavy heart. She seemed not to have heard my question, or perhaps she just ignored it.

'I also knew of your feelings for me,' she said, gripping my hand tighter, 'because I feel the same about you.'

I felt my heart leap in my chest - this was not the answer I had been expecting. Confessing her feelings for a man her father did not approve of? I suppose I had expected her to say very little, or become offended, but in the instant I decided to tell her, I knew I no longer cared what her father or anyone else thought.

'But, I… I got the impression your father does not approve?' I asked, overjoyed but confused.

'Oh, I know he does not approve,' she answered dispiritedly. 'My whole life I've needed his approval for every single, miniscule decision. Who I'm friends with, what activities I take part in, even the food I eat – everything runs by him. At times I've hated it, hated him, but I always found a way to cope with it, until now...'

I was startled to see that she was crying. Glistening tears ran down her pale face and fell away into the darkness beneath us. I did not understand what had upset her so.

'What... what do you mean?' I asked as I felt the sinking feeling in my stomach begin anew. Something was dreadfully wrong.

Meera looked away from me as she took a deep, shuddering breath. When she looked back, there was anger and despair in her eyes.

'Wolf... Takashi, I am to be wed against my wishes!' I felt as though I had leapt from the wall and the ground was now rushing up to meet me. 'My father has arranged the marriage and... and I can see no way out of it!'

'Who are you to marry?' I asked hoarsely, around an egg-sized lump in my throat. But I already knew the answer. I think I had known it all along.

'Oh Takashi, my love, I am to marry Shjin Kitano!' These last words I heard as though at a great distance. It all made terrible, obvious sense now. I had harboured my suspicions ever since seeing that look on Meera's face at the mention of Shjin's name - but this was far worse than I had imagined.

I was devastated, heartbroken, and in that moment I realised just how selfish I was. Here was Meera, trapped, desperate, scared, and all I could think about was myself. I wanted to comfort her, to tell her it would be alright, but no words would come. She put her head on my shoulder and wept bitterly.

'I do not love him, Takashi,' she said through her tears. 'Oh, I can see how it would be a good match, the lord's daughter and his right-hand man, but I have never even had the chance to get to know him. Of course I respect him, as a man and as a warrior, but my feelings belong to you, and my father will not allow that.' She looked up at me then.

'What am I to do, Takashi?' she asked. Her earnestness and grief cut through me, but try as I might, I could still find no words of comfort for her.

'Say something, please!' she asked plaintively, her tearful words only making the misery tear at me more fiercely. When I did not reply, she took my face in her hands and she kissed me. I am not ashamed to say that I had dreamt of our first kiss many times, but to me, in that moment, her kiss was that of a wraith or spirit, for our union was now hopeless and impossible.

Meera withdrew and stood up quickly, stumbling backwards in shame at her actions.

'I should not have done that,' she said tearfully. 'I am to be married and must honour the man who will be my husband. I am sorry.' She bowed to the floor before disappearing rapidly down the wall stairs.

Left alone on the wall in a ringing silence, I gave myself over to the misery that welled up inside me.

I cried until my already sleep-worn eyes were bright red and bloodshot. My body shook so violently that I almost fell from the wall, but I did not care. Why had I not said something to comfort her? Why had I not at least told her, in my own words, how I felt about her? I sat there long past the dawn, feeling that if Zian were to arrive now with an army at his back, I would gladly jump down from this great height to meet him.

It was the sound of galloping hooves that awoke me from my dark and miserable thoughts. It was the messenger, flying back to the castle at top speed and he did not look at all happy. What else could possibly have gone wrong?

I hurried down the wall steps, guilt pricking my mind, knowing that Meera had come this way only hours before. I wanted to get ahead of the messenger and so I headed straight for the castle in the third tier. I thought about checking on Kamari and Katsu, but decided that the news the messenger had was more important.

I had only minutes to wait outside the castle before the messenger hastened into view and I followed him into the main hall. As usual, Orran was already seated at the far end of the room and it seemed he had been dozing before the messenger burst in.

The man bowed low to the floor and quickly relayed his report.

'My lord, I rode non-stop through the night to reach Toramo and, even before I arrived, I could tell something was not right.' He took a deep breath and an angry glint flashed in his eyes. 'My lord, the village is deserted, and by the look of it, they left recently and in a hurry. There is not a single person left there. The honourless cowards have gone back on their word and have turned tail and fled. I followed their trail a short way and it seems that they have gone deep into the south, away from the threat of Zian and his army.' Orran digested this news sourly and his face twitched angrily.

'Then those traitors have left us little option but to attack with only the full force of the Kurai,' he said with resignation. 'We must leave immediately, for I fear we may already be too late.'

When I arrived at Katsu's house, I found Kamari was already awake and helping Katsu's mother Mila to prepare food. I explained the situation with Toramo to Kamari, but I did not say anything about what happened between Meera and I. I could see that Kamari was itching to pick up a blade and it was clear that the thought of another battle did not perturb him in the least.

Before leaving, I looked into Katsu's room and saw that he was still in the same state as yesterday. I felt terrible leaving him like this and would have felt much happier if he had been riding into battle with us, for I knew that above all things he wanted to be a strong Kurai soldier. But unfortunately, it was not to be. Kamari and I gathered our swords from Katsu's room and left for the main gate. I did not know it at the time, but once I left, Harakima would never be the same for me again.

The Kurai had massed by the front gate, many of them on horseback for the long journey ahead of us. I had assumed we would be marching with the lower-ranked Kurai until I noticed a young boy walking toward us, leading two horses. One of them I did not recognise - a black stallion with a fine, long mane and tail - but the other horse was far more familiar.

'Dagri!' Kamari said delightedly upon seeing the horse.

'We found him wandering outside the castle shortly after you were rescued,' the boy said. 'We've been feeding him up ever since and gave him some much-needed training on how to behave,' he continued with a small smile. 'But still, he's thrown many a rider who attempted to control him.' With a delighted smile on his face, Kamari climbed straight into the saddle and gripped the reins.

'Thank you for treating him so well,' Kamari said with a swift bow to the boy. 'He has been through a lot already, more than most horses would ever see in a lifetime.' The boy handed the reins of the other horse over to me.

'This is Jiko,' the boy said, indicating the black horse. 'Lord Orran wishes you to ride. May they bear

you safely.' We thanked the boy and prepared to leave.
I had ridden a horse only a handful of times before, but
that did not really seem important right now. The two
swords hanging at my side were loose and I tightened
them with trembling hands, but it was not fear that
made them tremble. I knew I should feel worried. I
knew I should feel frightened, even terrified. But I felt
none of these. All I could think about was Meera, and
all I could feel was despair.

The time was drawing closer and soon we would
have to leave. Lord Orran himself came down to
the first tier and spoke to the assembled men. It
was only now that I noticed how much older he
looked than our first encounter. Anxiety seemed
to have crippled him and the hair that had once
contained grey patches was now all but grey. He
told us that he would not be coming with us and,
looking at him now, I could fully understand this.
He looked as though he could barely sit a horse, let
alone ride or fight. His words gave us strength for
the battle ahead and when we left, we did so more
bravely than I would have thought possible. As we
exited through the main gates, we were waved-off
by the families of the Kurai warriors, as well as
many of the villagers, who came out to wish us well
and offer their prayers.

Each one of us knew that not all of us would
make it back, but we were yet to find out who would
return home and who would be lost along the way.

I will always remember the ride to Zian's fortress. You could not imagine a journey that seemed to take as long as this one did. Time seemed to dilate as we trudged steadily northwards. I think this feeling was due to the tension that every man felt. It was not fear exactly, for I was sure the Kurai did not feel fear like other men. But all the same, we would rather that the journey had gone by in a flash and we had got to the battle quickly, instead of it dragging-on for what seemed like days and prolonging the sense of unease.

Nobody spoke much. It may have been a Kurai custom to prepare oneself mentally, as well as physically, before a battle. As Shjin had told us, a Kurai lives as though he is already dead, so as to be of more use to his lord, for he will not fear for his own safety as much as any normal warrior. I felt now that I could almost relate to this; the crushing news that Meera had given me last night had left me feeling like a ghost.

As usual during quiet times, my mind flitted around, never settling on one thing for long. I remember thinking that I could not believe the people of Toramo had fled. Haratamo and the other Overseers had seemed so genuine in their offer of aid, but as it turns out, it was an empty gesture all along. I remembered the panic-stricken faces of the Toramo villagers and understood why they had not stood their ground and fought, but the warriors fleeing as well? I had thought that a warrior's honour was prized more highly than anything else and yet these men had turned tail and lost every shred of theirs.

Jiko bucked suddenly and whinnied. He had trodden on a discarded blade, presumably dropped by one of the foreign soldiers as they fled Harakima. I stroked his neck until he calmed down. He did not seem badly injured, although spots of blood could now be seen dotting the grass beneath him.

It was then that the weather began to get colder. It was almost imperceptible at first. The wind became icy and the Kurai soldiers pulled their kimonos tighter to keep out the chill. Soon, however, they had their heads bent against a wind that blasted their cheeks and froze the breath in their lungs. The grass beneath our horses' hooves was frozen and brittle, cracking beneath them. It was not long before a fine layer of snow stretched out northwards ahead of us, steadily deepening as we progressed onward.

'This is not normal weather for this time of year...' Kamari said, mystified. 'What is going on?' But to this question, most of us had already guessed the answer.

'Gorobei! Gorobei, you must look at this!' a man yelled from the front of the line. Gorobei rode smartly past us and caught up with the man, who had stopped some way ahead, by what appeared to be a large snowdrift. The men in front of us fanned out to allow everyone a closer look and, as I drew nearer, I felt the snow around us pervade my mind with icy terror. What had looked like a giant snowdrift was in fact, on closer inspection, the smashed husk of a small house. It looked as though winter itself had concentrated its malice upon it, for the house was almost entirely encased in ice.

'Over here, look!' another man shouted from further to the north. Soon, a second house was revealed beneath the snow, then a third and a fourth and a fifth, each appearing as though it had been carved from ice.

'It is an entire village,' Kamari breathed in horror. 'Completely destroyed by ice!'

'This was once known as Tiramai,' a soldier close by muttered to a younger Kurai warrior. 'They had been a protectorate of Harakima for years.' I had dismounted from my horse and was peering through the window of what had once been a small, homely looking building. What I saw through that window terrifies me still.

The body of a young boy hung suspended in the ice like some ghastly figurine, his expression frozen forever in an expression of horror and disbelief that made me reel back in shock. His limbs flailed in a grim snapshot of his final moments, as though he had been caught in a tidal wave before the water had frozen around him, and then I understood.

'Is there a lake or some other water source around here?' I asked a soldier standing nearby.

'There is a large lake known as Thormfi, not far to the north-east,' he answered, puzzled by the odd question, and in that moment the terrible truth was laid bare to me.

'It is Aralano, he has been released!' I said aloud, and the Kurai soldiers nearby turned to look at me. 'He drove the water from Thormfi Lake here and froze it in place, before the villagers had chance to flee!' There were fierce and worried mutterings amongst the men, but Gorobei stepped forward and silenced them.

'This is horrific news,' he shouted so that all could hear, 'and to be broken to us in such a way. These foreigners… these murdering barbarians must have used this village to test the dragon's wrath. We now know what we are up against, the horror we will soon face. I know none of you would consider turning back, but now we have proof of what would happen if we did,' he continued, indicating the houses with their frozen occupants. 'The dragon would surely follow us and we would watch our families freeze like these poor souls. We have no choice but to continue and confront whatever is before us.'

A sudden noise at the northern edge of the village made us prick up our ears and listen. It sounded as though several people were creeping stealthily away from us, their boots crunching in the deep snow. Before anyone could stop us, Kamari and I had left the others and hared off towards the noise with our blades drawn. The cold weather had worsened the wound in my foot and so I limped badly as I hurried to keep up with Kamari, the snow against my sandaled feet sending shivers up my spine.

There were seven of them. Perhaps they were part of some scouting party or rear guard; perhaps they had just come to see what they could salvage from the wreck of Tiramai. Whatever the reason, we had come upon seven foreign soldiers who had been attempting a quiet escape from the village.

With an angry snarl, Kamari and I charged into their midst. A weak sun had appeared from behind the clouds and it shone down upon my blade, chasing little diamonds of light along its edge as the tip found the first of the foreigners and ran him through. I viewed the stark contrast of his dark blood spraying the pearly snow through emotionless eyes. There was time enough for Kamari to bring down another of the soldiers before the Kurai joined the fray.

The remaining five barbarians were dealt with swiftly and it was not long before I was back in Jiko's saddle and we were continuing on toward Zian's fortress.

As we journeyed on, the snow gradually faded and vanished and, looking back the way we had come, the path of the water and the dragon was clear. Thormfi Lake was north-east of Tiramai and the ice and snow trailed off in that direction.

As I watched it dwindle into the distance, I wondered how long the area would remain in the grip of that unnatural winter, but I had no way of knowing. Perhaps the awesome power of the dragon would leave it like that forever, unaffected by time or the change of season.

For the rest of the day we rode without mishap, leaving the village of Tiramai far behind us.

Night drew in slowly and the shadows gradually lengthened. A wolf howled to our left from the fringe of some trees and I watched it slinking northwards between the trunks, as though it were following us. I blinked and shook my head – for a second it had looked like the wolf spirit I thought I saw on the way to Toramo that had looked like a man, but also strangely not so. But when I looked back it had gone, though somehow I was sure it had not gone far. I felt that it was still nearby, watching us; guiding us maybe.

It was around midnight, when shadows had blanketed the land, that we reached the fortress. It was an enormous, dark and imposing structure, surrounded by a moat that had not yet been filled with water. A massive drawbridge took up most of the front wall and in the gloom it appeared like a huge, gaping mouth, waiting to swallow us. It was a style of architecture unusual to this land, perhaps something Zian had picked up whilst overseas.

'How did they build this so quickly and without our knowledge?' a soldier nearby asked a comrade.

'Do you not know your history?' his friend replied. 'This is where Lord Hiran's fortress once stood before he was defeated by Lord Orran. The foundations of the building were ready and waiting for them.' I did not have much time to think on this for I could see shapes moving along the battlements and soon we all heard their barbaric voices raised in cries of alarm.

Other than the journey here, there was no build-up to this battle. There were no grand speeches, no theatrical shows of force; not even the time to feel fear. One moment we were sizing up the fortress for ways to attack, and the next we heard the hiss of barbed, and possibly poisoned, shafts hailing down on us. One such shaft struck Jiko in the shoulder and in a fit of shock and pain, he bucked me from the saddle before his legs gave way and he fell to the floor twitching. I landed badly on my injured foot and struck my head on the hard earth, but managed to stagger back to my feet. A man on horseback to my right was pierced through with an arrow and fell wordlessly from his mount, clutching at the arrow that stuck from his chest. Groggily, I looked around at the rushing, spinning figures surrounding me and at once felt very small and alone. What was I doing here in the midst of a battle of men? I had lived for little over fifteen summers and had spent most of that time with my books learning history and philosophy, not learning the art of combat like the Kurai soldiers around me. I was surrounded by trained soldiers, twice my age, in a battle that would in all likelihood take my life. But I did not have time for such thoughts. It looked as though the arrows were indeed poisoned, for Jiko was no longer moving. I heard the sound of many arrows arcing to meet me and rolled behind the body of the horse just in time.

With my eyes shut tight and my hands over my ears, I still heard the arrows strike his flesh and felt his body jolt into my back. For but a moment, the idea to remain where I was filled my mind. They didn't need me, the Kurai could deal with Zian's petty rebellion on their own. No one would have to know. I could hide here and no one would find me. I would be safe here, alone, lying amongst the dead.

But lying is what it would be; lying to myself that it would sort itself out, lying that I would not be found and killed, lying that I could even live with myself after... I could not stay here; young as I was, I knew the value of honour and I knew that staying here would let down not only myself, but those I loved. My family, Kamari, and of course, Meera.

With this in mind, I heaved myself up and looked over Jiko's carcass toward the fortress. It did not appear that the assault was going well. The Kurai had brought ladders with them, as the barbarians had done, but due to the dry moat, the ladders barely reached the battlements. Luckily, however, the fortress was not fully complete and in some places the battlements had not been finished. It was upon these that the Kurai concentrated, but it seemed that at every turn they were being frustrated. Kurai bowmen suppressed the foreigners on the wall top with well-aimed shafts, but every time the ladders were put in position, they were thrown down again.

I picked up a bow and quiver of arrows from a fallen Kurai and ran to join a group that were firing upon a cluster of barbarians trying to push over a ladder below them. I saw that Kamari was amongst them, loosing arrows in high arcs. I knelt at their side and notched an arrow to my bowstring. Together we managed to drive back the men swarming the ladder top and it seemed that the Kurai climbing it would make it over the half-finished battlements. But as the topmost Kurai warrior was about to climb off, a huge figure hurtled from the wall and grabbed hold of both him and the ladder. The force of his leap was such that the ladder fell slowly backwards and smashed into the ground killing both men instantly.

As time wore on, it became apparent that there was no way of breaching the fortress walls. We had killed many of their men, but as each one fell, two more would pop up in his place and we were running out of ladders. There seemed to be no way for us to gain entry.

And then something happened that seemed to surprise not only us, but the barbarians as well. All eyes turned to the drawbridge as, with a loud 'thunk' and a metallic squeal, it suddenly fell open, slamming into the earth on the far side of the moat in a shower of mud and dust, the chains that lowered it snapping taut with a dull rattle. For what seemed like minutes we all stared at it dumbfounded, completely taken aback at this sudden and unexpected point of entry.

Looking back at the wall tops, we saw that the foreign soldiers had vanished from their positions, and at once we suspected a trap. After a brief consultation, the Kurai regrouped and cautiously edged onto the drawbridge toward the open gateway and the empty courtyard beyond.

CHAPTER FIFTEEN

Everything was silent as we passed slowly through the gateway into the darkened courtyard – and that was what made us so wary. The men on the walls could not have gone far. But Gorobei had told us that, now we were inside, their numbers would be no match for us.

The courtyard beyond the gateway was vast and cobbled in grey stone, surrounded by buildings of differing sizes with doors that led off further into the fortress. The area was lit by pale moonlight and torches that blazed in sconces around the walls, but even in this light it was difficult to see if anyone was standing in the shadowy corners.

All of the mighty Kurai army had now entered the fortress and we stood in a huddled group with our weapons drawn and ready. There was not a sound to be heard anywhere, other than the heavy breathing of the weary warriors. It was as though the men we had been fighting only minutes earlier had disappeared into the ground.

'Why do they hide?' one Kurai soldier spat angrily, stepping to the front of the group. 'Are they scared now they don't have their walls to cower behind?' As his words died on the still air, a sound behind us made every man spin around. Without warning the drawbridge began to winch upwards. A few men ran forwards to try and prevent it, but it was no use. With a loud boom, the drawbridge closed completely and we guessed at once that it must have been a trap.

Every one of us stood flicking our heads from side to side and up and down, looking from the walls to the doors to the shadows, to see where the attack would come from. The tension mounted. Minutes passed and there was still no activity. It was as the man who had stepped forward began to edge back to the group that the first blood was drawn in this second clash. A heavy wooden spear was hurled as if from nowhere, impaling him through the belly and knocking him off his feet.

It was then that the true battle began in earnest. Men sprang up along the wall tops and poured out of every doorway to clash with the Kurai warriors. I had never witnessed anything so fierce and so bloody. Crimson rivers ran along the channels between the cobbled stones forming dank pools in which the moonlight reflected dully. Everything around me was a mad whirl of dull colour and roaring sound, it was like being caught up in a hurricane.

My blade weaved shapes before me, cutting down several men as I fought over to Kamari, who had joined a small group of the younger Kurai warriors.

We fought together until we found ourselves backed-up against a wall and hemmed-in by leering barbarians. There seemed to be no end of them. Some of the older Kurai saw our plight and rushed over to help us, breaking through the advancing ring from behind and driving them away. I took the opportunity of this brief lull to speak with Kamari.

'I'm going to search for the prisoners,' I yelled to him over the clangourous sounds of battle. He looked at me and nodded.

'Be careful,' he said as he signalled my intentions to the Kurai warriors we had grouped with.

Slowly but surely, we hacked our way over to a door through which the foreign soldiers had entered the courtyard. Before turning to enter, I looked into the melee of battle and saw the figure of Gorobei. He was crouching down on the floor in the shadows, away from the battle. I hoped that he had not been too badly injured.

I gripped Kamari's hand briefly then darted through the open door, just as three arrows thudded into the thick wood behind me.

Once inside, the sounds of screaming and clashing steel lessened and I felt able to think more clearly. If Gorobei was correct then my family, and other poor souls from the villages the barbarians attacked, must be somewhere in this fortress. I had to find them. I had to make sure they were safe. But it was not long before I was hopelessly lost in a maze of blank-looking stone corridors, each turn I took offering no clues as to where they could be.

I came across some stairs and jogged up them and soon found myself in what appeared to be the gatehouse above the drawbridge. Looking out of the small slit window confirmed these thoughts, but also showed me how the battle was going. Bodies littered the floor like broken dolls, scattered about carelessly. Blades whistled and arrows hummed and now and then terrible screams rose high above the din. I watched as men I had seen around Harakima fell before the foreigners and I longed to rejoin the fray.

Hoping to help the trapped Kurai below, I moved towards the winch that raised and lowered the drawbridge. It was large and sturdily built and, on closer inspection, I noticed to my consternation that it had been jammed in place. I spent a minute or two in vain trying to release it, but soon realised that I could not do it on my own. There was no retreating for the Kurai now, no easy escape; this was a fight to the end.

I hurried out through the other door of the gatehouse to continue my search for my family, but stopped short as a voice hailed me.

'W-Wolf, is that you?'

I could not believe it. It did not seem possible to have heard that voice here, now. I turned and looked down a corridor I had run past without noticing.

'Shjin?' I asked, looking down at the slumped figure. A knife was clasped in his shaking hands, hovering over his stomach, and with a shock I realised he had been about to commit ritual suicide. But it seemed that on the sight of me he had changed his mind, for the moment at least, because he lowered the blade.

'Yes, it's me,' he answered, his voice slow and laboured. He looked gravely injured. A dark red patch of blood was slowly spreading across his kimono from a wound in his side and his face bore the brunt of a merciless beating.

'What… what are you doing here?' I asked in bewilderment. And then at once it came to me, the only explanation as to why Shjin would be here, in Zian's Fortress.

'It was you,' I said, as cold fury stole over me. 'You stole Orran's Blade!'

'No, please, you must listen to me…' Shjin said desperately, but I would not let him speak.

'I knew there was something wrong, ever since I first told you of the barbarians' movements!' I shouted, hating myself for ever trusting him. 'Now I know what it was. It reminded you of what happened at Kenmui. All these years you've been waiting, just waiting for the right moment to take your revenge on Orran, and Zian offered you the perfect opportunity!'

'No, you've got it all wrong,' he cut in, trying to make his voice heard. 'That is not…'

'How could you do it?' I yelled in his face. 'Those men out there trusted you! They fought and died alongside you and all the time you were simply waiting for a chance like this!' I paused as hatred boiled-up inside me. 'You once told us what it means to be a Kurai warrior. Now I know your true self, I cannot believe you said those things so straight-faced, when all along they meant nothing to you!'

'You do not know the full story,' he pleaded, looking me straight in the eye. 'There is more to this than you think you know; you must let me explain!' I drew my sword and put the tip to his breast, placing a little pressure on the hilt so that it dug into his flesh.

'Speak,' I said harshly. 'But there is nothing you can say that can redeem you of this.' Shjin took a deep breath and it looked as though it hurt to do so. I could hear the breath rattling in his lungs as he inhaled.

'I suppose I should begin this where you did,' he said, easing himself into a more comfortable position with my sword point still on him. 'When you first spoke of the army's movements, you may indeed have seen something in me that you did not understand, for I was thinking deeply and I was greatly worried. But it was nothing to do with what happened at Kenmui. I do not blame Orran for what happened, nor do I blame Kichibei; neither wished for innocent blood to be spilt, it was simply a terrible coincidence that they met there.' He stopped for a moment, clasping his wound tightly and grimacing in pain. He continued. 'What I am about to tell you, no one else in Harakima has any knowledge of.' At this point he stopped again and it looked as though it was extremely difficult for him to continue.

'Wolf...' he began. 'I have a family in a small village north of Harakima, a family that Lord Orran has no knowledge of whatsoever and I... I feared for their safety.'

My heart beat faster as the implications of this hit me.

'You have a family!' I said aghast. 'But what about your arranged marriage to Meera?'

'I know, I know,' he said brokenly, his eyes damp, 'but Lord Orran thought it would be a good match and as his loyal servant I could see no way to escape the proposal without offending him.'

'Then why not just tell him about your family?' I asked.

'Because he did not give his permission for me to wed,' Shjin answered. 'To tell him about it would be to admit I went behind his back and married a woman totally unsuitable to my rank.' He looked past me through a window as the memories came flooding back to him. 'I met her one day when I was visiting the ruins of Kenmui. Her name is Lila and she lived in a village called Harani, not far from where Kenmui had once been and I suppose... I suppose she reminded me of the girl I had once loved in my youth. After I got to know her, I realised I no longer cared for the consequences and we were married in secret. We have since had four children together, all without the knowledge of Lord Orran. I visit them as often as I can; Orran just thinks that I am out on patrol.'

'So… so you do not love Meera?' I asked, hardly daring to hope at the answer.

'Of course I do not love her!' Shjin answered bitterly. 'But I am in the same position as she; I assume she does not love me either and neither of us can do anything to get out of this.' For the briefest of moments this revelation made me blind to his crimes, but then I saw it all clearly again.

'So, you have a family,' I said, adding extra pressure to the sword hilt. 'That still does not explain why you would take the Blade and risk the lives of everyone you know!' Shjin did not flinch as the blade dug deeper.

'As I said, I was worried about my family and then… and then, shortly after I first spoke with you…' Here he paused and his face twisted suddenly with anger and grief, and with his fist he pounded the hard stone floor. 'No man should be made to endure what I have suffered!' Tears were now streaming down his face and desperation seemed to take hold of him completely. 'Shortly after we spoke a carrier bird arrived, bearing a note and a small parcel containing… containing, oh Lila! Containing her ring finger, still bearing the ring I gave her!'

The sword clattered from my limp grasp. I finally realised what Shjin had gone through and what had driven him to do this. However, I could not begin to understand the kind of torment he had suffered since the day I first met him. His dual loyalties to his family and his lord must have torn him in two. Seeing him in this state, I had not the heart to feel any anger towards him. How must it have felt to keep bottled-up the knowledge that your family are being held captive and tortured?

'In the end I could stand it no longer and told Zian I would do it,' Shjin said, his voice subdued and almost inaudible. 'He sent me my orders, told me an attack was planned on the main gate to cover the theft and my escape. When I was away from Harakima I blew a horn and that was the signal to end the attack. I took the Blade to Zian and he told me he would release my family. I had planned to try and take back the Blade once they were free, but Zian expected this.' A grim smile curled the corners of Shjin's mouth as he thought of it. 'Zian was as good as his word; he released my family but threw me in a cell in their stead.'

'But why did he choose you, out of everyone in Harakima?' I replied.

'He chose me because I am the highest-ranking soldier in the Kurai,' Shjin answered. 'I am one of the few people who can even get near the Blade Room, let alone inside it. He had also found out about my family. I have no idea how he found out, but he did, and he knew he could use them against me.'

'So, what are you doing up here?' I asked, looking around us. 'Why are you wounded?'

'I knew that Orran would have no choice but to send the Kurai to reclaim the Blade,' Shjin replied, sitting up and adjusting the grip on his wound. 'When I heard the sounds of battle I pretended to choke and the guard came in to check on me. I managed to overpower him and made my way to the gatehouse. Everyone was on the walls at that point, so I was able to lower the drawbridge to let you inside. Of course, once I lowered it the guards came and found me. One of them stabbed me and left me here to bleed out. They waited until you were all inside before closing the drawbridge behind you. I do not know their numbers, but I wanted to help in whatever way I could.' He shifted position slightly and his face creased with pain. 'I have lost my honour. I have helped the enemy and betrayed my lord; I should kill myself in shame.'

'You cannot kill yourself now,' I said, handing him a sword and picking my own up off the floor. 'You can still regain your honour. You may think it is an honourable death to take your life, but is that not just the easy way out? The only way to truly regain your honour is to put right your mistakes and serve your lord until the spirits themselves take you… you should not go looking for them.' I tried to help him to his feet, but he pushed me away and raised himself off the floor. Once standing, he looked into my face as though seeing me for the first time.

'Ever since the day we met, you have been a constant surprise to me, Wolf,' he said, a faint smile tugging at his lips. 'Wherever your parents are, I'm sure they are very proud. You should go on ahead.

I'll catch up.' I looked at him and the knife that lay at his feet, doubtfully. Noticing where I was looking, he chuckled. 'Do not worry, I promise I will follow you shortly.' With one last look at him, I hurried away from the gatehouse and out on to the wall top.

Out on the wall top, the clamour of battle washed over me once more. Several torches had been knocked to the straw-covered floor in the courtyard below and the heat from the fires stung my eyes, as hot ash drifted lazily past me.

As I hurried along the walls, my thoughts consumed with locating the prisoners, I did not notice a man standing on the wall top and ran right into him, knocking him shrieking to the courtyard below. It was one of the foreign archers and at the sound of his fall the other archers lining the walls turned to face me. They had been caught unawares and I did not waste a moment. At such close range they could not use their bows effectively and their only other weapons were small machetes, which they quickly drew. I cut down the first of the archers before he could raise his weapon to deflect the deadly blow. He toppled lifeless from the wall and crashed into the cobbles with a sickening crunch.

The narrow platform I stood on made it impossible for more than one of them to attack me at a time and I used this to my advantage. Their short machetes were no match for my blade and one by one, I sent them from the walls, where they were no longer a threat to the Kurai. One of them managed to gash my shoulder as he fell, but I could not stop to think about this. Only when every one of the archers had fallen did I allow myself to take a breath and lean against the wall to my right.

The gentle pressure of a blade in my back made me freeze, my sword still held in my hand. My heart sank. I had come this far only to be caught taking a breather in the middle of battle. I dropped my sword, hoping that my attacker would get complacent and give me an opening.

'I knew I would find you,' a familiar voice said. 'I had to find you. You left without saying anything and I knew then you did not expect to come back... or did not want to.' Meera! She had followed me here, but how and why? I whirled around to face her.

'After the last time we spoke I knew that nothing would change unless I made it change,' she said breathlessly. 'I just couldn't take that life any more. The rules, the schedules, the aching, crippling boredom of having every step of my life planned out for me. I want to make my own decisions! I want to make my own mistakes! I want to ride and fight, take risks and travel far – I want to live my own life! And, Takashi... I want to live it with you! I do not care what my father thinks any longer, we will... we will run away together! Just run and see where our legs take us! You are all that I need.'

Meera sheathed her sword and there, high above the chaos in the courtyard with the sounds of death all around us, we kissed, and her touch was no longer that of a wraith. Her touch will stay with me, long after I pass from this world, and her words… I will never forget them.

'But, how did you get out of Harakima?' I asked, gazing into her face.

'With the help of Ellia,' she answered, looking down into the courtyard. 'My father tried to stop me from going. I think, somehow, he knew I would try to run away with you. He locked me in my room, but Ellia set me free; she is down there somewhere now, fulfilling her dream to fight alongside the Kurai.'

I had almost forgotten where we were, but at these words I looked down into the courtyard to see how the battle was going.

'Oh no,' I whispered, and Meera gripped my hand tightly. It looked as though Gorobei's estimates of enemy numbers had been wrong. Well over half the Kurai soldiers lay dead or dying and those that remained were cornered by an ever-growing horde of foreign barbarians. They continued to fight bravely against overwhelming odds and, to my relief, I saw that Kamari was still alive, battling hard on their left flank, but it did not look like they could hold out for long. It seemed that Aralano would not be needed to conquer the Kurai after all.

It was as all hope faded and the foreigners closed in ever tighter, that a figure stalked along the wall top towards us. It was Gorobei!

CHAPTER SIXTEEN

Shadows obscured Gorobei's face, but what I could see of his expression showed a malevolence that frightened me. But Meera seemed not to notice this as she turned and spoke to him.

'Oh, Gorobei! I am glad you're alright,' she said, looking down at the destruction of the Kurai, 'but what are we to do, there does not seem to be much hope.'

'There was never any hope,' he spat back mockingly as he advanced towards us. 'You should not have come here.'

'Gorobei, what is wrong with you?' Meera asked, taking a step back. 'We must do something to help them!'

'No,' he answered with a sneer, 'I have already done my part in bringing them here.'

'What do you mean?' Meera asked fearfully. 'Please, do not come any closer!' There was a sigh of metal as Gorobei drew his sword from its sheath and continued to prowl along the battlements.

'My job was simple,' he replied, coming to a stop in front of us. 'To make the Kurai think their numbers were more than a match for Zian's mercenaries. It wasn't difficult, Orran has always been an arrogant buffoon, and as you can see,' he continued, pointing down at the beleaguered Kurai, 'his over-confidence will be the end of them.'

'But, why? Why would you help him?' Meera asked, bewildered. 'Those men are your friends, people you have known for years!'

'Hah, you have no idea what Zian offered me,' he said, his eyes narrowed to slits. 'He showed me what could be mine.' I could see the greed shining in his face; the lust for wealth and power. 'Our foolish country has lived in the dark for so many years, shutting itself off from the rest of the world, oblivious to the goings-on in distant lands. But Zian showed me what we have missed in our ignorance. The dragon was the key of course. With Aralano at his command Zian could seize control of the entire domain, but that is not all the dragon is good for, oh no.' He licked his lips and his face glistened with sweat in the moonlight. 'You have no idea of the worth of a single dragon tooth overseas, it is astronomical! But, of course, Orran would not know this - the fool has outlawed all dealings with foreigners.'

My blade was on the floor by my feet, but I knew he would cut me down before I could reach it.

'When Zian's men found us near his fortress, Zian himself came to me. He had known of me at Harakima, told me that if I helped him… I would share in the profits and the power. But if I refused to help him, I would join the dead and the Blade would be taken anyway.'

'But you offered Lord Orran your life in shame,' I said, stalling for an opportunity to grab my sword.

'I knew he would not accept it,' Gorobei answered jeeringly. 'The service I had performed in bringing the information was too great. And anyway, that pretence only strengthened my cover and my honour in his eyes.'

'But what about the Toramo warriors,' I asked, hoping to keep him talking as long as possible. 'What if they had joined us and swelled the Kurai ranks?'

'Yes,' Gorobei replied ponderously. 'That could have posed a problem. I tried to push Orran to attack swiftly with only the Kurai but he would not hear of it. Luckily, however, those cowards at Toramo fled, leaving him with no choice.'

Behind me, I could feel Meera shaking with rage. Gorobei noticed this and sneered.

'Your father is a fool,' he said, addressing her directly and raising his weapon. 'A fool, and a coward, too old and feeble to join his own men for an honourable death.'

It was but the work of a moment and neither I, nor Gorobei, had expected it. But no, that is a lie. All along I knew Meera had strength in her, and coming here tonight through all this death and destruction only proved that.

Faster than I would have thought possible, Meera ducked from behind me and picked my sword off the floor. Before Gorobei could move a muscle, she had grasped the hilt firmly in both hands and driven the sword into his belly, the tip exiting through his spinal column in a shower of blood and tissue. He looked stunned and confused as she withdrew the blade. Then his features went slack as he slipped from the wall, his great bulk smashing through the roof of a burning stable and disappearing into the flames.

The last of the Kurai were soon to fall and I began to contemplate joining them and sharing their fate. It was drawing towards morning but it seemed to get darker still as each Kurai fell before the barbarians' blades.

Meera put her arms around me and rested her head on my shoulder as we prepared to climb down and meet them.

At that moment a high-pitched sound rang out from the south and I froze, listening intently. I began to think I had imagined it until the sound was repeated, this time closer, and everyone below us stopped to listen. Together, Meera and I ran to the southern end of the wall and looked out across the flats.

The sight that met our eyes made us throw up our arms and cheer. An army, the size of which I had never before seen, was heading towards the fortress, tall banners fluttering in the early morning breeze, and at their head were two people on horses I recognised easily - Haratamo Motsoshige and Daisuke Inaba.

I was about to head to the gatehouse to try to lower the drawbridge when, as though at the mere thought of it, the drawbridge began to slowly descend. It was Shjin, it had to be! He must have seen them coming and managed to un-jam the winch. I rushed back to the centre of the wall and shouted down into the courtyard, where all activity had stopped.

'An army has come to help us! Take heart and fight on, Zian has not beaten us yet!' Waving their weapons in the air with a defiant roar, the remaining Kurai hurled themselves at the mercenaries and drove them backwards with the ferocity of their attack.

With Meera leading the way, we ran as fast as we could down the wall steps and into the courtyard. Side by side, we carved a path through the chaos to join the Kurai, who had been filled with renewed vigour. In the maelstrom of combat we came upon Kamari, fighting back to back with Ellia Kishitani. Kamari had been cut in many places and a deep wound on his brow was bleeding into his eye, forcing it closed, but he battled on regardless. We joined them and formed a square, whirling around and around, cutting into the ranks of the mercenaries and holding them off until help arrived. And it was not long before it did.

Soon, masses of heavily armed men were swarming into the castle through the gateway and I cheered along with the remaining Kurai. At first the barbarians seemed to dither, unsure whether to try to fight these newcomers or flee. But they had only one option, as Orran's force had been left with. The only entrance to the fortress was now blocked and there was no other way to escape, save from throwing themselves off the battlements. So, with waning courage and the single desperate urge to live, the barbarians confronted this new army.

I spotted Daisuke amidst the crowd and, together with Kamari, Meera and Ellia, we cut a path around the outside of the battle towards him. He was fighting from his horse and causing devastation amongst the diminishing ranks of the enemy. When he spotted us he reared up his horse and its front legs lashed out, kicking a barbarian backwards, then he wheeled around and approached us.

'Wolf, I am glad to see you,' Daisuke said as he reined his horse to a halt. 'And Meera too, I thought I might find you here.'

I looked at this man with newfound respect. Only hours previously I had suspected him of betraying Lord Orran. Now I knew the truth, but not the whole story.

'I see you have been busy,' I said, looking at all the men he had led to Zian's fortress. 'Where have you been these past few days? The last time you were seen was at the Blade Room...' He did not answer right away. He glanced at all the men fighting grim battles around us before turning back to speak.

'I was not at the council when this was discussed but I found out from my sources that it was Zian who commanded this foreign army,' he began. 'I am not sure if you know this, but I was somewhat friendly with Zian before his exile...'

'We were aware,' I answered with a wry smile. 'It did not help your case...'

'I imagine it didn't,' he replied dryly. 'As long as I knew him, Zian had always had an interest in the Blade. That interest became a passion and that passion grew to obsession until I no longer recognised him.' Daisuke broke off for a moment and looked away, as memories crowded his mind. Finally, he looked back to us.

'When I heard he was back, I knew he would have returned for one thing, and one thing only,' Daisuke broke off again as a barbarian lunged at him. Wheeling around he swiftly dispatched the man before turning back to us.

'Perhaps this story can be saved for...'

'Please,' I cut across him. 'I must know what happened.' Daisuke sighed and continued, faster now.

'Fine, but I shall be brief – my sister has a family in Toramo and I feared for their safety when Orran refused to move quickly against Zian. When his forces attacked Harakima, I was terrified it might already be too late and resolved to visit Toramo at once, but first I went to the Blade Room to check enough guards were stationed. There I met Shjin...'

'Who was forced to steal the Blade for Zian...' I cut in again.

'Yes, we worked that part out, a letter was found in his quarters...' Daisuke said distractedly, staring out into the fray. 'Anyway, I left Harakima and rode to Toramo only to find it deserted. I imagine Lord

Orran assumed they were cowards… far from it. They went south to ensure the safety of their young and elderly and to recruit more fighters to the cause. I joined them south of Agrath's Deterrent where we managed to recruit several groups of masterless warriors.' Daisuke was clearly itching to get back to the fight and his last few words were rushed.

'When we made it back to Harakima with an army at our backs we discovered what had happened and followed you immediately, and now… here we are.'

'Hey, did you come here to talk or fight?' Kamari said to Daisuke with a sardonic smile. As if in answer, Daisuke expertly dispatched an axe-wielding barbarian who had snuck up in Kamari's blind spot.

Kamari snorted with laughter at this, then, as one, we turned and launched ourselves back into the fray.

I could not tell you how many men I killed that morning as the sun rose in the east, but what I can say is that I feel no remorse for their deaths. So much innocent blood was on their hands that death was the only thing left to them. I suppose in the end it is a belief; my belief, and I believe that for every action there is a consequence. Those men were thieves and murderers who had spent every moment of their vile lives taking from people. Their consequence was to have their lives taken from them.

Morning was drawing on and the din of combat was gradually diminishing. It was as the last of the mercenaries were being dealt with that a sound we all feared was heard emanating from beyond the northern mountains, growing ever louder. It was a petrifying and demonic sight that met us as we turned slowly to face it. I could try to describe what I felt, but it would fall far short of the numbing terror that latched onto every inch of me.

What I saw winging its way closer that morning has been engraved on my memory ever since. An unmistakeable shape, straight from a nightmare, could be seen silhouetted against the clouds, flying swiftly towards us, his wrathful roars causing even the sturdiest heart to quail.

It was Aralano.

Aralano was coming.

CHAPTER SEVENTEEN

I could see him quite clearly now in the pale light of dawn. I had read many books on the legends of his kind and confirmed his identity at once as a Water Dragon, one of the rarest of his species ever thought to roam this land. His body was long and thin; almost snake-like in appearance, though he had four legs that were tucked close to his body while in flight. His wings were wide and set high up his body, the membranes thin but strong. He was a deep midnight blue and would have been completely camouflaged, had he attacked a few hours earlier. From either side of his snout, two thick, trailing whiskers whipped about in the breeze as he closed in on us. On his head were a pair of short, curved, jet black horns and his eyes were purest white, but for the small slit-like pupils at their centre. His tail was barbed with vicious-looking spikes, similar to the horns on his head. In short, he was a magnificent beast, and all the more terrifying for it.

The men under Daisuke's command had wasted no time upon seeing Aralano. Within seconds, his archers had lined the wall tops and formed ranks in the courtyard, while others readied throwing spears and those with neither held their swords ready. Soon, everyone was in position and the fortress became still, as every eye tracked the hellish form growing steadily larger in the morning sky. For what felt like hours the only sound to be heard was the beating of Aralano's wings, but then his furious roar split the silence as he prepared to visit vengeance on mankind. It was man's fear and paranoia that had led to the destruction of his kin, that had driven him to madness; and now they would pay dearly for their mistakes.

In an instant he was above us and his freezing breath rained bitter spears upon the men below, the cobbled ground erupting in gleaming shards of ice to form deadly barriers between his earthbound opponents. It became unbearably cold, so cold that my hand stuck to my bow grip, but if we surrendered to it, then all was lost. I kept in a close group with Kamari, Meera and Ellia and as one we fired arrows into the dragon whenever he passed over. On more than one occasion we only just escaped being caught by his breath as it blasted icy paths close by us.

Many men succumbed to Aralano's fury that morning and were frozen where they stood, never to move again. Some he only winged, freezing an arm or a leg in place, only so he could return a moment to later to finish the job. The same thing almost happened to me. I could see him snaking through the sky towards us, but I stood my ground and drew back my arrow for the shot. The others had already begun to dodge and I knew he was too close, but still I waited.

It was as he was inhaling to breathe on me that I fired. I watched as the arrow tore a ragged hole through his wing and listened to him squeal in pain. I threw myself to one side but I had waited too long and his breath caught me, freezing three of the fingers on my left hand. As he soared away, I looked at my fingers and saw that they had already turned blue and were starting to turn black. They were stiff and rigid and it was agony to bend them. I could still just about hold a bow but it was extraordinarily painful to do so.

However, it was starting to look as though bows would no longer be needed. When Aralano next passed over, I could see that his wings were filled with gaping holes and I could hear the wind whistling through these tears. A spear, hurled by one of the Kurai, ripped through his wing and with that the membrane gave way under the pressure, tearing apart until it was nothing more than tattered fragments of dead skin. Aralano wobbled in mid-air, tried and failed to maintain his balance, and with a roar, began to fall to earth.

The noise he made as he hit the courtyard was deafening and the ground shook beneath our feet with the impact. Half blind with pain and fury, Aralano uncoiled himself and reared up from the hollow he had smashed in the cobbles. Shrieking in anger he shot a hail of ice in a wide circle around him, drawing the battle lines in this next phase of combat. His long, blade-like claws soon came into deadly effect as he began swiping at any who ventured near him. Brave and foolish men were cut clean in two as they sought to pierce the dragon's hide, but none could get close enough to do any real damage.

I was standing alongside Kamari on the outer edge of the dragon's range when I noticed something out of the corner of my eye. I knew I could not afford to be distracted, but some instinct screamed at me to look at the main building of the fortress. I did so and there, at a second-floor window, stood a man I thought I recognised, but I had no idea why... He was there for only a second before he vanished back into the depths of the building and I found myself gripped by the sudden and uncontrollable urge to follow him. Before I could stop myself, I had begun walking towards the fortress, but at a surprised shout from Kamari I took control of myself again; I could not just leave my friends out here.

Aralano was showing no signs of weakening. Even as more and more arrows pierced his thick skin, he continued to slash ferociously at the brave souls advancing on him and breathe icy jets at any within his range. A gasp arose from some of the men nearby and I looked around to see what had startled them. A lone figure had staggered from a doorway by the dragon's haunches and was approaching him fearlessly, a spear clutched in his hands. Shjin? What was he doing? He would get himself killed!

I ran forward, closely followed by Meera, unsure whether I was going to stop him or join him. Amazingly, the dragon seemed not to notice Shjin's approach until he was almost directly beneath him. Then, incredibly, Shjin hailed the dragon. Aralano looked around in surprise and then narrowed his eyes wickedly at the sight of this man who had dared to come so close.

Aralano lowered his head until he was almost level with Shjin. His gaping maw split in a hideous sneer as he inhaled deeply to freeze his impudent foe where he stood.

But before he could do so, Shjin drew back his arm with lightning speed and hurled his spear, fiercely and accurately, and it found its mark. The metal spear tip punctured the dragon's eyeball and drove deep into his head with the awful sound of metal on bone. Blood bloomed from the wound and spattered the ground as Aralano reeled backwards, his ear-splitting bellows of pain driving every man in earshot to their knees.

In his suffering, the dragon thrashed around, his fearsome claws scoring countless grooves in the cobbled floor and smashing gaping holes in the walls. In anguish, he stumbled forwards and too late I saw the danger I was in. His great claws were swinging towards me and I knew there was no chance I could escape. With my end drawing near, I thought of Meera, and waited for the blow to fall.

But that blow never came, and frequently... I have wished that it had. Instead, a blow of a different kind hit me. I felt a body bulling into me, knocking me backwards and out of the path of danger. My head cracked the floor and everything went blurry.

From my position on the ground I saw a figure arc past me and crash into the wall, crumpling to the floor in a limp heap. With my head pounding, fit to burst, I dragged myself over to the body that lay still and silent on the cobbled stones. I drew close and held the head between my hands, ignoring the excruciating pain in my frozen fingers. The features floated serenely before my eyes and I could not see clearly who it was. But then I heard her voice...

'Takashi, my love.'

'Oh, no... no, no, no.' From her prone position Meera looked up at me, but only her eyes moved for her neck had been broken.

'I followed you here,' she said with difficulty, tears in her eyes. 'Now you must follow me. I will be waiting for you.' Her eyes were closing against her will but she managed to keep them open. 'Kiss me...'

'I... I cannot see you,' I whispered back, tears falling down my cheeks.

'You will,' she said. I bent my head and kissed her gently and as we kissed I felt the throbbing in my head lessen. Slowly, her face came into focus and I looked once more into her eyes.

'I wanted us to run away together,' she said, her voice faltering. 'And I believe one day we will. We will run together, my love.'

'I love you with all my heart,' I answered, hardly able to speak the words. 'I will find you again.'

Meera's face slackened and her eyes began to close. As I watched them shut for the last time, my sight blurred by tears, I saw something moving deep within them. A shape could be discerned there, deep in those recesses; though I did not understand it at that time.

'I know I will find you again,' I repeated, as those beautiful eyes closed completely, and forever.

CHAPTER EIGHTEEN

I laid her head gently on the floor, then rose slowly with my sword in hand, my eyes now dry of tears. Numbly, I walked toward the blinded dragon who had slumped down, clutching his face in agony. Kamari told me of this later, though I had no idea at the time, that at that moment I had looked more like a wolf than a man, as though another part of me had risen to the surface. And I believe him. This was a part of me I had been unable to understand, a nagging pull toward the unknown that had frightened me, but now I embraced it willingly.

The few remaining Kurai who had witnessed Meera's passing joined me as I advanced upon the dragon. They had all known and respected Meera and felt the pain of her loss, though none as deeply as me. They saw their chance with the dragon lying crippled and goaded by her death, they attacked.

I had thought Ellia would have been amongst them, having known Meera since childhood, but instead she had rushed to the body and was cradling her dear friend in her arms, weeping brokenly.

As many swords and spears stabbed at him, Aralano lashed out blindly, catching many men with his claws and sending them careening backwards, never to rise again. But his strength was now all but spent and his attacks became slower and more laboured. Gradually his head sank to the floor and our chance finally came. Together with Kamari and three others I rushed to the dragon's side, narrowly avoiding a last-ditch attack, and hacked at his thick neck until it was almost completely severed, and finally he went still. Silvery-blue blood spilled from his wounds to spread slowly across the ground at our feet, its opalescent surface reflecting the weak morning sun.

A great cheer went up from the men all around me and weapons were raised high in victory. But I could not join them in their excitement. I had lost too much and it was still not over yet.

When I think about Aralano now and recall the story of his life before imprisonment, I often feel pity for him. He was driven to this maddened, wrathful state by the destruction of his kin, only to have his rage bottled and stoppered for use as a weapon against others. He was the last of a great line of beasts that would still walk this earth if their paths had never crossed with man. It was our hatred and fear of the unknown that had brought about the doom of all dragons, a pattern that is all too familiar with our race.

Like one in a dream, I beckoned to Kamari and he followed me to a door leading into the main building of the fortress. Before we could enter, Shjin caught up with us, limping badly and clutching at his side.

'There is still Zian,' I said simply, my voice dull and hollow to my ears.

'Then we will find him together,' Shjin said, leading us through the doorway.

The main building was no less confusing than the gatehouse I had entered earlier. Doors and stairs led off in every direction and so we worked our way up slowly, checking every room we passed for any sign of Zian. I began to fear he had already fled and the thought that he might escape made me tremble with anger. We had almost reached the highest room in the fortress when we finally came upon him. He was kneeling with his back to us, staring out of a window that overlooked the courtyard. In his trembling hands he held Orran's Blade, the tip of which hovered over his stomach. In horror, I realised that he was about to escape me by committing ritual suicide, and I could not let it happen.

At the sound of the door opening Zian looked round, his face gaunt, and at last I recognised him. He looked much older than he probably was, as though he had aged very quickly in a short space of time. His greying hair was tied in a long ponytail and he had a short black beard that failed to hide the many wrinkles scoring his face.

That face. It was the face I saw when I shut my eyes. The face I saw when I lay awake at night. The face that had caused my lack of sleep all these years.

'It was you,' I said aghast, as that hated face looked at me with confusion. 'You murdered my grandfather!' His voice was reedy and spiritless when he answered; the voice of a broken man.

'What are you talking about, boy?'

'Ten years ago, you rode into Aigano on horseback and cut down my grandfather in front of me,' I spat, moving closer to him. 'He had been yelling something when you killed him. What did he try to tell me? Why did you murder him?'

Zian looked at me with the unconcerned, disconnected eyes of a man who has accepted his fate.

'I'm sure I have no idea what you...' he began.

'Liar!' I screamed at him. 'You know precisely what I mean – why did you kill him?'

At first, Zian looked bewildered and as I drew closer he raised the blade even further, ready to stab himself, but I could tell that he was thinking hard. Then, as the mists of memory cleared, it all came back to him.

'Ah yes, now I remember,' he said, looking at me more closely. 'That was a long time ago, are you still bitter about that?' he added with a chuckle.

'Tell me,' I shouted, stopping as he made a motion with the blade.

'Your grandfather was simply in the wrong place at the wrong time,' Zian said nastily, but with little conviction. 'I met him at the port of Kagashi where he was selling your surplus crop. Well, I suppose "met" is the wrong word. He overheard me speaking to someone about my intentions for Orran and his pitiful Kurai and immediately set off for Harakima on his horse. Fortunately, in his haste, the old fool went entirely the wrong way and ended up heading towards Aigano instead. I must say he gave me a good chase, right across the domain before I finally caught up with him at your village. It was fortunate indeed that only you were there to witness it.'

'Then why did you not kill me too?' I hissed venomously.

'I am no monster,' he replied, looking me up and down. 'I was not going to kill a little boy.'

'But you would have a dragon do that for you?' I asked, thinking of Tiramai and the destruction that had been wrought there.

'Just so,' he replied. For a while I was at a loss for words, my hatred of this man was so great that I could not think clearly. So many thoughts collided inside my head. There were so many things I wanted to say to this vile man, but one question bubbled to the surface.

'Tell me this,' I said, taking a step closer. 'After going to the trouble of stealing the Blade, why not send the dragon against Harakima?'

Zian snorted mirthlessly.

'I assume that loud-mouthed idiot Gorobei told you more than he should,' he answered looking out of the window at Aralano's corpse. 'It was the dragon's teeth I was most interested in and I was not going to risk them unnecessarily when I had an army of greedy, empty-headed mercenaries at my disposal. Those teeth were worth far more to me than the lives of some honourless foreigners.' His body sagged as his gaze swept the courtyard and his decimated army. 'Now everything is in ruins,' he continued, his face hardening. 'I have no choice. I will take my own life in shame.' Without a moment's pause, Zian brought the blade plunging down towards his belly, but I was now close enough to intervene.

'You will not deny me,' I yelled, gripping his wrist and knocking the blade away. For a moment we struggled and I was unable to bring my sword into play. I managed to get my arm around his throat, but he headbutted me on the chin, clacking my teeth together and almost making me bite through my tongue.

With bursts of light popping before my eyes, I watched him scramble across the floor towards a blade by a stack of books. He held this aloft and approached me, poised to strike. I gripped my own sword and circled him, dazedly rubbing my eyes. He charged in, recklessly swinging his blade and hoping to catch me while I was stunned, but I managed to deflect the blow. As he passed, I kicked him in the back, sending him head-first into the wall. He got unsteadily to his feet and came at me again, swinging even more wildly than before. I felt a feral growl erupt from my throat as he took a mighty swipe at me and I saw the fear gleaming in his eyes. I parried the blow easily and sent the blade spinning from his hands where it stuck point first in a small table in one corner.

Zian collapsed to the floor beneath the window and without hesitating, without even thinking about what I was doing, I rammed my sword into his chest. In the heat of the moment I had not noticed that Orran's Blade lay on the floor by his groping hand and as I forced the blade further and further into his body I saw his arm move in a blur, spending the last of his strength, and felt the blade enter my side. But I was not done yet. I clung onto my sword hilt until I knew he was dead and his arm slipped from my side, dragging the Blade out with it. Only then could I stop. Only then could I rest.

I crumpled to the floor, feeling my blood draining from me, and finally gave in to the sleep that had so long been denied me, and for a long time, I remembered no more.

CHAPTER NINETEEN

When I awoke, I wished I had not, for where I had been there were no worries or doubts; no fear or pain or grief, nothing to remind me of the terrible loss that consumed my body and soul. I wanted to sink again, back down into that place and be lost there forever. There I could forget; there I could forever avoid the memories of what led me to this place.

But it seemed that the peace and solitude of that place would be denied me. Even though I gave myself up to it completely, I was unable to find it again. I was shut out from there now and would have to face up to the awful feelings inside myself.

Slowly my eyes opened and a familiar room was revealed to me. It was a room in the Healing House, the very same room I had awoken in when I first arrived at Harakima. This time, however, I was alone. Kamari was nowhere to be seen. I hoped he was alright and nothing had happened since my fight with Zian.

I tried to sit up to get a clearer view of the room, but the pain in my side made me yelp and fall back to the mat. I looked at the fingers on my left hand

and saw that the three hit by Aralano's breath were withered and dead-looking. I could still move them to some degree, but it felt strange, like they were no longer a part of me.

Somewhere nearby, I could hear a flute playing. It was a slow, mournful tune and the long, quavering notes only deepened the despair I felt. I could tell the person playing it had suffered a loss as I had. Perhaps we were both mourning the same person; but I would never know for sure.

I heard footsteps approaching and the door slid open at the other end of the room. Two people entered – two people I had feared I would never see again. At the sight of me lying with my eyes open, a bowl of water was dropped to the floor with a crash and they rushed to my side.

'Oh, Takashi, we have barely left your side and now you wake while we're out! How do you feel? We have been so worried about you!'

Against all the odds, they were here, now, alive and unharmed, a lifeline to my shattered soul. My mother and sister knelt by my mat and put their arms around me, hugging me tightly, but careful to avoid my wounds. I felt stronger at the sight of them and for the moment at least, I no longer wished to return to the silent place I had awoken from.

'It's so good to see you,' I said, with a pained smile. 'How long have I been here?'

'You have been asleep for six days now,' my mother answered, drawing away from me and holding me at arm's length. 'At first we feared you would not pull through, you were slipping away from us slowly, so slowly… like you wanted to leave us.' She was weeping now, with relief and happiness, but also with sadness, knowing the dreadful things I had witnessed. 'I am so happy you are alright; I don't know what I would have done if you had got away from us, Takashi.'

'Please, don't call me that,' I said, the words coming unbidden from my mouth. 'That name and that life are dead to me.' I was not sure who had spoken those words. It was as though another part of me had taken control, perhaps already was in control; but I welcomed this part with open arms.

'Then… what should we call you?' my mother asked perplexed.

'Wolf,' I replied, looking through the window behind them, 'that is the only name I now recognise.'

For an hour or more I spoke with my family and they told me all that had happened to them since the raid on Aigano. They had been discovered in our home by the mercenaries and were dragged off, bound and gagged, in the midst of their horde with the rest of the captive villagers. They had been forced to march for days at a pace they could barely keep up with until they finally arrived at Zian's fortress and were put to work. Since then they had been making weapons and armour, cooking food, hauling stone and weaving cloth; whatever their taskmaster forced them to do under threat of the lash.

They had been locked in small, cramped cells during the night and thrust back out to work at the crack of dawn. This had been their daily routine for weeks. And throughout these weeks they heard nothing of the goings-on in the domain; no news reached their ears and, for all they knew, Orran had already been overthrown. Most of them had given up hope of rescue until the night they heard the first sounds of battle, and their hopes were finally reignited.

They also told me they had met a man named Mauru and his family. He had told them about discovering Kamari in the mountain pass, his slow recovery from grief and the terrible attack on Kirina. Despite myself, I smiled at the thought of the look on Kamari's face, knowing that Mauru and his family had survived their harrowing escape after all.

My thoughts turned to Kamari and I asked how he was and whether he was coping with everything that had happened. They told me he had only recently left my bedside to attend to some "important matters", but would tell me nothing more until Kamari himself arrived. He had been injured during the fighting, though nothing too serious, and so had been up and about for the past few days.

I was beginning to feel more myself and was chatting with my sister when the door slid open without announcement. Lord Orran stood in the doorway and behind him I could see the woman I presumed to be Lady Orran, though I had never set eyes on her before. They stepped into the room and I could see at once the enormous similarities between mother and daughter. It was almost more than I could bear to look upon her and I had to turn my head for fear of crying out in grief.

Lord Orran bade my mother and sister leave and, as they left, I saw my mother give Orran a look that was warning, even threatening, but he paid her no heed. The door slid shut and for several minutes the room was silent. The silence dragged on, the minutes stretching out before me, and I began to wonder why they had come, or if they even knew where they were. Then Lord Orran spoke.

'My daughter is dead,' he began, looking me in the face but not appearing to truly see me, 'and it is because of you we mourn her loss when we should have been celebrating her wedding.' It would have been better if he had struck me or just killed me where I lay. Lady Orran gave a great choking sob and clutched her husband's arm.

'Dear… no,' she murmured, tugging at his sleeve, begging him to say no more. But Lord Orran would not be silenced. It was obvious he had been waiting to say this to me for some time.

'I tried to do what was best for her, I tried…' Orran said, his voice rising sorrowfully. 'When I couldn't stop you riding out to fight Zian, I locked her in her room.' He was pacing the floor now, speaking more to himself than to me. 'I did it for her, everything I've ever done I did for her. She needed to be stopped, she needed to be contained… she needed to be protected from you! But then she broke out and followed you anyway...' Here he stopped pacing and turned furiously to me. 'You... you led her to her doom!'

'No!' I answered tearfully, trying to believe my own words. 'She went because she wanted to fight!'

'She went for you! She went for love!' Orran replied angrily. 'If you had never come here she would still be alive. Don't you see? I arranged her marriage to keep her safe! She did not love Shjin, she would not have followed *him* to her death. I hoped that by marrying her to Shjin she would finally settle down and forget these ridiculous ideas of joining the Kurai.' Orran took a step nearer and thrust his ashen face inches from my own. 'If she had never met you, she would still be alive, safe and well with her family, here in Harakima where she belongs!'

Without warning, Lady Orran slapped her husband mightily across the face, taking him completely by surprise.

'Let him be,' she said forcefully, and before he could say any more, she led him from the room, leaving behind a ringing silence.

I turned onto my side and wept anew for Meera; for the guilt I now felt over her death. Was Orran right? Would it have been better if I had never come to Harakima or had died during my journey here? After hearing Orran's impassioned words, I could no longer see it any other way. It *was* my fault she had died.

Oh Meera…

'For days after I met you, I had no idea if you felt anything for me,' I whispered to myself. 'Then, that night, when I learned you were to marry Shjin and all seemed hopeless, I suppose… I suppose, yes, however it occurred… I did not want to return to Harakima. I had no idea you would follow me and I wish that you had not. I wish I had simply never made it back here…' I stared unseeingly at the ceiling as tears blinded me. 'You are the only person I will ever love. I know some day I will meet you again, but it will not be the same, and it will not be soon enough.' I buried my face in my blanket and gave vent to my feelings and I did not see anyone else for the rest of the day.

The next morning, Kamari bounded into my room early and grasped my hand in friendly greeting. It was unusual to see Kamari out of bed at this hour and I wondered what could have excited him so. Perhaps his bed was on fire.

'I hope no one has told you yet!' he said excitedly. 'But I am to marry Ellia Kishitani as soon as you are well enough to attend!' He was beaming happily and I was glad to see that he was able to rise above all that had happened to him; to us.

'Congratulations!' I said, trying to sound more enthusiastic than I felt. 'Have I been asleep so long that so much has happened?'

'You have been asleep longer than even I would have thought possible,' he answered with a smile. 'And much has happened, yes. Ellia is to be made a Kurai! It is said to be extraordinarily rare for a woman, but her bravery during the battle earned her the right to join what remains of those noble warriors. I had never spoken to her until after the battle. But since then I have been unable to leave her side and, just yesterday, I plucked up the courage to ask her and she accepted my proposal!' I could not help smiling at the look on Kamari's face, his laughter was infectious. 'And you will not believe who we found among the prisoners, Mauru and his family!'

'Yes, I heard from my mother,' I said, still smiling. 'I am glad they are alive.'

'We also rescued everyone who was captured at Aigano,' Kamari went on eagerly. 'And when they saw who saved them and discovered what happened, Takash... I mean Wolf; their respect for us was reborn! I understand it now - their resentment, their hatred even; but that has been wiped clean! We have earned their respect; that is something I should have realised sooner.' I could have told Kamari I had known this all along, that I had meant to tell him dozens of times, but I did not want to spoil his mood.

'So come on, get well quickly - I am not sure how long I can hold off marrying her!' He slapped me heartily on the back and I winced, but in his merry state he did not notice and left the room with laughter on his lips. I was about to try and go back to sleep, for I at last seemed able to sleep normally, when Kamari came back into the room. He looked anxious and sorrowful all of a sudden.

'In my excitement I did not stop to think how you must be feeling,' he said shamefully. 'I am truly sorry about Meera's death and I know that my happiness at finding Ellia may only make your pain worse. If I have offended you then I hope you will accept my apology, and I hope you know that I will always, always be there if you ever need me.' I nodded my thanks to him, feeling that I could not wish for a better friend than he. 'Meera's funeral, along with the others, will of course take place before my wedding,' he added. 'They are waiting for you.'

There was still something I needed to ask him before he left.

'What is to happen to Shjin?' I asked, for even after everything that happened, I felt I understood why he did what he did and would hate to see him punished for it. 'Has anything been said? Is he to be forced to commit ritual suicide?'

'I do not know much, but I believe Lord Orran is at a loss for how to deal with him,' Kamari answered. 'What he did was terrible, but Orran understands he was in an impossible position and his years of loyal service may just wipe the slate clean. However, Orran has, at least temporarily, dismissed him so that he may search for his family, as they were not found at the fortress. He has already left, but he wished you a speedy recovery and says that you will cross paths again.' Kamari moved to the door, but turned as he got there. 'Get some rest; I want you up and about as soon as possible for the wedding.' With a parting smile he left and I turned on my good side and fell into a deep, dreamless sleep.

By the next morning I felt strong enough to leave the Healing House and the funerals could finally take place. I was still unsteady on my feet and Kamari had to support me so that I would not fall over. I had aggravated the wound in my foot during the battle and was limping worse than ever, and the damp weather made the pain in my deadened fingers intensify.

All of the fallen Kurai were to be burnt on individual funeral pyres and these were arranged in long lines in the second tier of Harakima. For each of the warriors a small and intricate model wolf had been made out of folded paper. This was then placed on their chests by their folded hands. This, I learned, was another part of the old Kurai legend surrounding the wolves. These paper tokens were said to help guide the spirits of the fallen into the skin of a wolf, so that they may ever remain a guardian of the domain.

Meera's body had been laid on one such funeral pyre. She had been dressed in a simple white kimono with her hands clasped at her breast. I had been given a paper wolf to set on her body, because, when it had come down to it, Meera had been a warrior, braver than any I had ever known. Her mother and father stood near her body, but I could not bring myself to look at them; I could not face their accusing eyes.

I placed the wolf gently on her chest and bent to kiss her forehead. She looked as beautiful in death as she had in life and it was hard to accept, as it always is, that she was truly gone.

An attendant had begun to move down the row, setting the pyres alight. I did not want to witness her body burn but some instinct kept me rooted to the spot, watching as tongues of red-orange flame slowly engulfed her body. As I stared into the fire, tears spilling silently down my cheeks, a hazy, flickering form appeared, dancing in the flames. A wolf's head looked out at me, proud and noble, staring straight into my eyes. I recognised those eyes and saw the love burning within them. In that moment it all became clear. Images crowded my mind - *the wolf and his dead mate, the wolf spirit, the shape in Meera's dying eyes. I now understood why they had seemed so significant. I finally knew what I had to do.*

I glanced up then, knowing what I would see, and sure enough, there it was. The wolf spirit sat some distance away, watching the pyres burn. Its eyes met mine and I nodded faintly at it, then turned back to Meera.

'I will find you again,' I whispered quietly into the fire. 'One day we will run together my love.'

A couple of days later, the celebration of Kamari and Ellia's wedding was held and a more joyous occasion I have not seen. The food and wine were plentiful and the company good, but I felt apart from everyone there and could not bring myself to join in. I laughed and joked with Kamari whenever he could tear his eyes away from Ellia, but I knew I had to leave soon. I knew she was out there and I had to find her.

There were few Kurai left now after Gorobei's horrific deceit, but many of the men recruited from the south had volunteered to join Orran's army and serve him loyally. But the Kurai were not the mighty army they had once been.

Kamari came and sat by me with a half-full jug of rice wine and shook my hand warmly.

'I do not blame you for not joining in,' he said, plonking his jug down on the table, 'and I can see that you want to be left alone, but I need to talk to you.' He waved his arms about, drunkenly indicating the castle around us. 'Harakima is all well and good, my friend, but this is not our home is it?' He paused for a moment as he belched loudly. 'Ellia and I are thinking, well… we will stay here for a time, but we are thinking then of returning to Aigano and rebuilding it. There are many who will join us - the original villagers of Aigano, the prisoners whose villages were destroyed, some of the people from the south… We would build it again, greater than before, and, using Ellia's new status as a Kurai, become an outpost of Harakima. And… we want to do this with your help.' I had suspected he would say something like this. I had in fact been thinking a lot on this subject while I had lain abed these past few days.

'Kamari, my friend, you know at any other time I would go with you anywhere,' I said, staring out to the north. 'But, this time… I cannot.' He looked shocked and puzzled and so I went on. 'I know you do not believe in this… I know you do not believe people can come back. But I feel… I *know* that she is out there. Her spirit is too strong to simply leave this world. She is out there somewhere, waiting, and I will find her.' I did not know if he would understand, if there was even a way to make him understand, but after a few moments, he nodded in quiet comprehension and his acceptance of my path only made the bond between us stronger. For the rest of the celebration we both remained quiet and subdued and spoke very little.

My mother was less than happy about my decision to go, but I believe, deep down, she understood my reasons. She worried constantly about how I would feed myself and where I would shelter, and all I could do was promise to take care of myself. She had decided to take Mia and join Kamari and Ellia on their mission to rebuild Aigano. I told her I would return there one day and, by the look in her eyes, I knew she believed me.

And so it was that one cold, dreary morning I found myself standing outside Harakima's main gates looking back at my friends and family. At my side stood Dagri, heavily laden with food and equipment, and I hitched up the twin blades that hung from my belt. My mother rushed to me and gave me a last farewell hug, then disappeared back inside the castle, trying and failing to hide her tears. I bade farewell to everyone else, coming to Kamari last. We embraced as brothers and I promised this would not be the last time we spoke.

'I know it won't be,' he replied, with a half-hearted smile. 'I will come and find you myself before I would let that happen!'

With one final nod at Kamari I turned and left, heading off southwards and waving over my shoulder. I had not gone far when a voice hailed me and I turned to see Lord Orran walking quickly towards me. My first thought was that he had come to blame me one last time, but I was mistaken. He stopped before me and put out a hand to stroke my horse. For a moment or two he said nothing and simply stared unseeingly ahead.

'I ask now that you forgive me,' he said at last, his voice low, humble. 'The last time we spoke, I said many things in my grief that were untrue and unfair.' He looked at me and I could see a proud light in his face. 'I believe... have always believed, that everything happens for a reason; nothing in this life is without its purpose. Maybe you were supposed to come here; maybe she was supposed to follow you. The spirits have plans for each of us, but some, it seems... have greater purposes. Like you... and

Meera. You have been preserved, Wolf, and that can only mean that there are still greater deeds for you to perform.' Orran took a shuddering breath as he looked out across his domain.

'My daughter was a warrior; I had always known it. I had seen that fire before and knew where it led. I was scared... so scared for her that I... I never let her live, but by caging her I only pushed her further away. I blamed you for her death, but I do not really believe that and I could not let you leave still thinking it. If anything, it was I who drove her to this. In the end, all I know is that you loved each other deeply and there is nothing more good and right and without guilt or shame than that.' He had been staring into my face and when he realised what he had been doing, he looked quickly away. 'Well... I have said what I wanted to say. Also, I wanted to give you this.' He handed me a small and beautiful necklace that was wrought in the shape of a she-wolf. 'That was Meera's and it belonged to her mother before that. Take it, and take care of yourself, Wolf.'

He turned his back on me then, but stopped after only a few paces. Without turning his head, he said, in a low voice: 'If you should indeed find her... please... tell her... that I'm sorry... and that I will always love her...' His shoulders heaved and, without another word, he headed back towards the castle. I stared at the necklace for a while, then undid the clasp and hung it around my neck.

Turning on my heel, I set off and soon crested a low rise where I looked back at Harakima. Orran's words had raised my spirits a little, but I still had a long journey ahead before I would ever be able to return here. I held Dagri's reins tighter as I led him off into the light rain and mist, my sights set southwards and my thoughts far, far away.

EPILOGUE

Wolf put down his quill pen and rolled up the parchment he had been writing on. It had taken many months to document his story, but it had not been a wasted venture. With each fresh page he wrote, he felt his grief diminish, each word lessening the weight in his chest.

He was sitting in a rocky glade in a stretch of woodland and had been writing on a flat stone before him. Dagri stood some distance away, tied to a tree, contentedly chewing grass. Over the past few months, Wolf had moved from place to place, eating and sleeping where he could and writing whenever he had the chance, but above all, searching, always searching, for her.

He had run into trouble with thieves and bandits on several occasions, but had quickly seen them off or cut them down with the swords he still carried at his side.

He stood up then, for he had grown tired of this place and wanted to move on. As he packed his things back onto Dagri, he heard a sound coming from the trees behind him, the snapping of twigs, a faint rustling; something was drawing near.

With a hiss of steel, he unsheathed his blade and crept silently towards the sound, entering the shadows between the trees. Up ahead, a patch of sunlight filtered through the tree canopy, painting a bright circle on the forest floor.

As he approached it, the sound suddenly ceased and he drew to a halt on the outskirts of the light. His eyes scanned the treeline, his body tensed for any sign of attack, but what he saw made his arms go limp and the sword fall from his grasp.

A wolf stepped out from the darkness and into the patch of light. It stopped and turned to face him, fixing him with its piercing stare.

He recognised those eyes, those eyes he had come to know and love so well.

'Meera…' he whispered.

The Hirono Chronicles
will return with
Wolf Warriors

CPSIA information can be obtained
at www.ICGtesting.com
Printed in the USA
LVHW042240210920
666689LV00024B/966